"Come here and let me touch you..."

His grin was pure mischief.

Fran glared at him. "I can't stay here long," she pointed out. "I don't have any suntan oil on."

Martin stretched out on the raft. "We should have brought some with us. I'll time you so you don't burn." He glanced at his waterproof watch. "Five minutes to a side."

"You're such a thoughtful man," Fran said with exaggerated sweetness. "When you want to be." She lay beside him and began to feel the warm rays of the sun.

"Come closer," Martin said.

Fran's heart was beginning to pound. "I can't get much closer," she protested.

"I can," he said....

Dear Reader,

Although our culture is always changing, the desire to love and be loved is a constant in every woman's heart. Silhouette Romances reflect that desire, sweeping you away with books that will make you laugh and cry, poignant stories that will move you time and time again.

This summer we're featuring Romances with a playful twist. Remember those fun-loving heroines who always manage to get themselves into tricky predicaments? You'll enjoy reading about their escapades in Silhouette Romances by Brittany Young, Debbie Macomber, Annette Broadrick and Rita Rainville.

We're also publishing Romances by many of your all-time favorites such as Ginna Gray, Dixie Browning, Laurie Paige and Joan Hohl. Your overwhelming reaction to these authors has served as a touchstone for us, and we're pleased to bring you more books with Silhouette's distinctive medley of charm, wit and—above all—*romance*. I hope you enjoy this book, and the many stories to come.

Sincerely,

Rosalind Noonan
Senior Editor
SILHOUETTE BOOKS

SRRL-7/85

NORA POWERS
A Woman's Wiles

Published by Silhouette Books New York

America's Publisher of Contemporary Romance

For my father,
who gave me the idea
for this story
and his loving support over the years

and for my mother,
whose constant love and caring
have made so much difference in my life.

SILHOUETTE BOOKS
300 E. 42nd St., New York, N.Y. 10017

Copyright © 1985 by Nora Powers

Distributed by Pocket Books

ISBN: 0-373-08391-2

First Silhouette Books printing October 1985

10 9 8 7 6 5 4 3 2 1

America's Publisher of Contemporary Romance

Printed in the U.S.A.

NORA POWERS

taught English at the college level while working on her Ph.D. A prolific writer, she is the author of some five hundred pieces of children's verse, fifty-eight short stories, nine novels and various newspaper articles. She has been a published author for the past twenty years and reports, "I don't even recall how I started writing, I was so young."

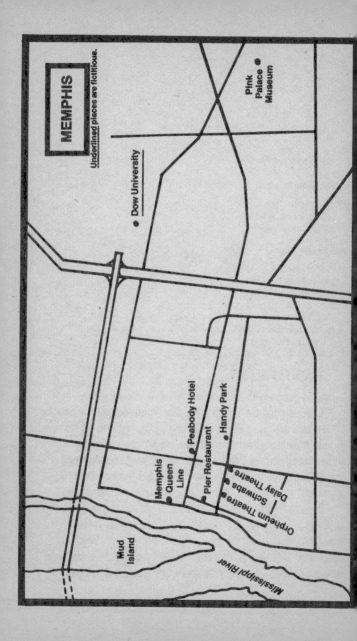

MEMPHIS

Underlined places are fictitious.

- Pink Palace Museum
- Dow University
- Memphis Queen Line
- Peabody Hotel
- Pier Restaurant
- Handy Park
- Orpheum Theatre
- Schwabs
- Daisy Theatre
- Mud Island
- Mississippi River

Chapter One

Fran Warren tugged at her powder blue jacket and frowned. Mr. Pettigrew's brilliant idea of having her carry a copy of her own book so that he could recognize her did not seem so brilliant now. In fact, it seemed ridiculous.

She felt slightly foolish, standing in the aisle of the airplane, juggling a carry-on bag, her purse, and the book. For now she kept it hidden in the crook of her arm. There was no need to have the book jacket prominently displayed, as Mr. Pettigrew had requested, until she was actually getting off the plane.

It was not that she was ashamed of her book. It was a good solid work, soundly researched and well written. It had helped innumerable women set their lives in order. But the title made Fran shudder. It was true it was catchy. What woman could resist looking at something called *How to Catch a Husband: The Scientific Way to Love and Marriage*?

It was not the title she had chosen, of course. That one had been much more academic, as befitted a serious work by a licensed psychologist. But, like the footnotes she had labored over, it had been discarded. For the sake of sales, she'd been told.

Fran's frown deepened. The whole thing had been a difficult experience for an essentially shy person. If she had known beforehand exactly how difficult... But, fortunately, she hadn't. Her book had helped many women; she was sure of that. The advice it gave was sound and helpful. She had a whole bulging file of letters from satisfied readers to prove it.

So perhaps all the uproar and personal upheaval had been worth it. Still, she had never expected such results: the title that sounded—there was no denying the fact—cheap and sensational; the cross-country publicity appearances on local television stations; the invitations to speak, to teach, to do any number of things.

She had turned down many of them, of course. There was her practice to consider. But she had also accepted some of the invitations, and had even grown almost to accept what the conservative part of her mind insisted on referring to as her "notoriety."

Actually, this invitation to go to Memphis to teach a two-week course in writing how-to books had seemed rather interesting. It also gave her an opportunity to visit with an old friend, and to have a little breathing space away from the cares of her patients.

With effort she held back another sigh. She should have let Harriet meet her plane and talked to this Mr. Pettigrew later. But the director of the Writers' Conference had insisted on giving her the red-carpet treatment.

Well, she thought as the passengers began to deplane, she would let Pettigrew get her settled and then she could call Harriet. She had come into town a day early so she could spend some extra time with her old friend from college days, and she intended to have it.

She frowned as she thought of the only other person she knew in Memphis. Her former fiancé, Ashley, had moved to the city a few years ago, Harriet had told her. Fran hoped fervently that she would not be unfortunate enough to run into him. Although she had gotten over Ashley, the memory of his leaving her for someone else still hurt. After all, she did have her pride. But enough of that, she thought firmly. Harriet was the only one from the past she was going to see.

Fran smiled to herself. She looked forward to this visit with Harriet. Harriet was fun, or at least she always had been. Outrageous fun, sometimes. School had not been a serious endeavor for Harriet. Her life's goal had always been clear to her. It consisted quite simply of finding a husband. She had already found two, but, as neither of them had proved to be Mr. Right, she was now in the market again.

Fran suppressed a little shudder. She had never liked using the terminology of business to describe personal relationships. But it was becoming more and more common. Everyone these days was talking about "investing" themselves and wanting a "sufficient return."

By this time she was coming off the ramp into the waiting room and she shifted the book so that its brilliantly colored jacket was clearly visible. Now, what did Mr. Pettigrew look like? From their phone conversations she was rather familiar with his voice, the raspy, fussy voice of a man who saw each detail as a mountain to overcome. It seemed miraculous that he had ever survived the number of conferences he had told Fran he'd directed. But her training had taught her that some people lived perpetually on the edge of disaster, and, indeed, were not satisfied to live otherwise. Mr. Pettigrew obviously enjoyed the series of minor crises that allowed him to lead such a harried life.

Fran abandoned her analysis of Mr. Pettigrew's character and continued to look for the man. As they had arranged, he, too, was carrying a copy of her book. She bit her bottom lip to keep from chuckling as she spotted him.

He was somewhat larger than she had envisioned—medium-sized rather than small—but his face showed the lines of constant strain, and the fingers that clutched her book worked spasmodically while the pale blue eyes under wispy eyebrows scanned the incoming passengers.

When her presence registered on him, he did not step forward immediately. Instead, he turned over the copy of her book that he held and stood there, comparing her face with the one on the book jacket.

"Mr. Pettigrew?" she asked as she reached him.

"Miss Warren?" In person his voice was even more raspy and his whole body projected an air of high tension that seemed incongruous for a man of his size.

"Yes," she replied, since he seemed to be waiting for confirmation. "I'm Fran Warren."

"Good to see you, Miss Warren. I hope you had a pleasant flight."

She had not. In fact, her head was beginning to ache, and she just wanted to be left alone, but she nodded. "Yes."

"Good. Good." He hovered around her like a mother hen.

"Now, we'll just go get your luggage and then I'll escort you to the campus." His hand on her elbow moved her along. "On the way I can brief you."

He sounded like a high-class diplomat, Fran thought, hiding the beginning of a smile. Or a director of a top-secret spy ring. "I didn't realize this was such an important conference," she observed.

Mr. Pettigrew stared at her in surprise. "Our Conference on the Bluff is known all over the country, Miss Warren. Every year we get the best possible writers to work with our students." He drew himself erect. "We have a reputation to maintain."

"Of course, Mr. Pettigrew. Of course."

They found her luggage and Mr. Pettigrew, ever in charge, loaded it into a smart black Cadillac. "It's furnished by the school," he said with pride, when he noticed how closely she surveyed the elegant vehicle. "We like to do things right."

Because you have a reputation to maintain, she thought wryly, but didn't voice the words. Experience had taught her that it was best just to go along with men like Mr. Pettigrew unless she had some strong objection.

So she climbed into the Cadillac and did not ask him why his very prestigious school didn't also provide a driver. There were, after all, limits beyond which reasonable guests did not go. Still, she wished she had avoided this meeting. The temperature in Memphis must have been over ninety degrees. Her blue suit had begun to go limp in the short time it took to get into the car, and as he pulled away from the curb, a blast from the air conditioner made her shiver.

Mr. Pettigrew did not notice. "Now," he said, his eyes on the road ahead, "we can talk."

"Yes," Fran replied, wishing again she'd arranged to stay in Harriet's apartment rather than on the campus where the conference was being held. Part of the charm of these things, though, was the chance for the students to mingle with the teachers, and to see them around campus after class. So she had invited Harriet to share her room at the school rather than going to stay with her old friend.

"Enrollment is fine. All the classes are full," Mr. Pettigrew was saying. "There's just one thing we have to worry about."

"And what is that?" Fran inquired, wondering what minor difficulty Mr. Pettigrew had chosen to upset himself with.

"Martin O'Brien."

Mr. Pettigrew pronounced the name in a way that gave rise to images of Attila the Hun pillaging the countryside. "And who is Martin O'Brien?" Fran asked, striving to sound duly impressed.

Mr. Pettigrew stared at her. "You don't know?"

"No," Fran said impatiently. "I'm afraid I don't. I've never heard of the man."

Mr. Pettigrew shook his head and Fran was reminded of someone's aged grandmother deploring the current condition of the world. "Martin O'Brien is a local TV interviewer. Our Golden Boy." Mr. Pettigrew's tone made it quite clear that he didn't share the general opinion toward the man. "He hosts the city's biggest talk show, 'Martin Says.'"

Mr. Pettigrew sighed deeply. "They say the networks have all been after him, but he's refused their offers. Claims he likes it where he is and doesn't want to leave Memphis."

Mr. Pettigrew's opinion of such foolishness was evident by the shaking of his graying head of hair. "They say he could work any place in the entire country, but he prefers to stay here."

"He must have his reasons," Fran said, already becoming intrigued by this strange man who disdained national prominence. What kind of person could he be?

"I'm sure I wouldn't know," Mr. Pettigrew replied disapprovingly. "I can't understand such a thing at all. Not at all."

They drove several miles in silence while Fran gazed out at Memphis through the car window, absently noting the cactus growing in front yards, the wrought-iron decorations on many homes, and realizing that everything here was low to the ground and spread out.

"This is the new part of town," Mr. Pettigrew said, noticing her interest. "Later on we'll go by some magnificent old houses, including the Pink Palace."

The name was intriguing, but Fran wanted to get Mr. Pettigrew back on the subject of Martin O'Brien. "Why is Mr. O'Brien apt to be a problem?" she asked.

Mr. Pettigrew stiffened, his hands tightening on the wheel. "I have never in my entire life known such an obnoxious man. He has no sense of class. No manners, even." Mr. Pettigrew came close to snorting. "He attacks his guests. Nothing—nothing whatsoever—is sacred to the man."

It was clear to Fran that a man like Mr. Pettigrew would resent questions, even legitimate ones, about his carefully laid plans. "Does he disapprove of the conference?" she asked. "Did he indicate that when he interviewed you?"

"Interviewed *me!*" Mr. Pettigrew turned pale. "The man *never* interviewed me. Never. I would not permit such a thing. It's you he's going to interview."

"Me!" Fran felt a jolt of anger mix with her apprehension; she was thoroughly tired of being raked over the coals, of having her theories picked to pieces by people who had no idea what they were talking about. She swallowed a sigh. "I suppose I can be interviewed like the others."

Mr. Pettigrew gave her a look that could only be termed compassionate. "He doesn't care that..." He snapped his carefully manicured fingers. "About the others. He just wants to talk to you." He gave her a worried sigh. "I presume you know how to handle these types. Your book is rather controversial, I suppose."

"Yes, I suppose so." Fran swallowed still another sigh. "Don't worry, Mr. Pettigrew. I've met this type before. Obnoxious is the word for them. When is the interview scheduled?"

Mr. Pettigrew shifted uncomfortably in his seat. "The man wouldn't say. He's a perfect barbarian. He wants to have lunch with you tomorrow. Then he'll set up the interview." He turned worried eyes on her. "I'm sorry to ask this of you, Miss Warren. We've held these conferences for many years and the man has never bothered us. Unfortunately, this year he has changed his mind."

"It's not important, Mr. Pettigrew," Fran replied. "Don't worry about it. I'll handle Mr. O'Brien."

Mr. Pettigrew looked about to disagree, but something in her voice, or in her expression, seemed to reassure him. "I suppose you're used to this kind of harassment," he said plaintively.

Fran nodded reassuringly. "Yes, Mr. Pettigrew, I am." She did not bother to tell him how she had forced herself to stand up under the verbal attacks of some of the country's most scathing TV personalities. The important thing was that she *had* learned and she felt confident that she could field any questions Mr. O'Brien threw at her.

"Why does he want to have lunch with me?" she asked. "That doesn't seem to fit the picture."

Mr. Pettigrew's lip curled in disapproval. "He fancies himself something of a ladies' man, I'm afraid. And he saw your picture on the book's jacket."

This time Fran couldn't contain her sigh. These were the worst kind: the ones who were so pleasant at first, playing little man–woman games, and then turned on you during the interview.

"What if I refuse to have lunch with him?" she asked.

Mr. Pettigrew almost slammed on the brakes. "You can't!" he cried. "That is," he amended hastily, "I hope you won't. O'Brien doesn't like to be crossed."

Fran's earlier image of O'Brien surfaced again. "He sounds like Attila the Hun."

Mr. Pettigrew's chuckle was dry. "I imagine that is rather how some people perceive the man, Miss Warren." He shuddered delicately. "As I said before, he has no class, no sense of propriety. One can appreciate wit, even a certain amount of sarcasm, where such is called for. But O'Brien..." He shook his head. "O'Brien comes at one with a bludgeon. The only recourse seems to be a counterattack." Again he cast her an anxious look.

"Don't worry about me, Mr. Pettigrew," Fran said rather grimly. "This time the marvelous Mr. O'Brien has met his match."

Mr. Pettigrew seemed relatively satisfied by this and turned his attention to telling her stories of the men who had built Memphis and had once occupied the stately, majestic old homes they were presently passing.

The campus of Dow University looked cool and shaded, but the summer heat was intense and Fran felt herself wilting again as they stepped out into it.

"This way," Mr. Pettigrew announced as he carried her bags toward an ivy-covered dormitory. "Your room is all ready."

Fran nodded. The sooner she got away from Mr. Pettigrew, the better she would feel. It was hard on the nerves to be with someone who was always expecting the worst, even though she understood that this had nothing to do with her.

The room was pleasant enough and blessedly air-conditioned. Fran gratefully breathed its coolness. It was small, of course, as dorm rooms always were. But it would be comfortable enough for the next two weeks.

Hot and perspiring and feeling that her clothes were stuck permanently to her skin, she could think only of getting into the shower. But she forced herself to wait patiently while Mr. Pettigrew inspected the room. She had no idea what he thought he might find, but she knew that trying to hurry such a man would be pointless.

Finally, he finished and turned to her. "Everything seems to be in order," he said, almost as though he regretted it. "But here is my card. Feel free to call me at any time. I live nearby."

"Thank you, Mr. Pettigrew." Tired as she was, Fran tried to put some cordiality into her voice. "I don't imagine I'll need anything, but thank you."

Mr. Pettigrew's forehead, which already seemed furrowed, grew even more so. "And you'll be able to

handle Mr. O'Brien?'' he asked anxiously. ''The conference can use publicity, but not the adverse kind. I
mean, we have our reputation to protect.''

''Yes, of course, Mr. Pettigrew. I understand that
perfectly and I'll do my very best. I've met men like
Mr. O'Brien before and I know how to deal with
them.''

Mr. Pettigrew did not look convinced. ''I can't im-
press too strongly upon you this man's devious nature.'' The conference director's sigh was monumental
and it was only with the utmost effort that Fran kept
herself from smiling at his theatrics.

''Not only is he devious,'' Mr. Pettigrew continued
as Fran tried to inch him toward the door, ''but he's
also considered very attractive to women. Very attractive,'' he said again, his pale blue eyes resting
speculatively on her face. ''He's one of those devilish
black Irishmen with masses of black hair and liquid
brown eyes. Has one of those new style of mustache,
too. The bushy kind. It's rumored,'' he added, looking at her hair, ''that he particularly favors blondes.''

It did not take a degree in psychology to hear Mr.
Pettigrew's dislike or to realize that much of it probably came from envy of Martin O'Brien and his
successes.

Fran remained calm. ''I really don't care what he
looks like,'' she said firmly, trying to ease Mr. Pettigrew's obvious apprehension. ''I've been interviewed
by all kinds, and I assure you I'm fully capable of
withstanding such a creature.'' She bit her bottom lip
to contain the small giggle that rose when she realized
that she was beginning to sound very much like Mr.

Pettigrew. "And now, sir, if you don't mind, I'd like to wash up and rest. Memphis in July is a little warm for a northerner. Will you be at the opening class tomorrow?"

"Probably not," Mr. Pettigrew replied as he finally took the hint and began to move out the door. "But I'll see you at tomorrow evening's reception. And of course, I'll be at the party at the Peabody Hotel later in the week."

He stopped suddenly and Fran suppressed a desire to shove him out bodily. The long ride, the heat, and Mr. Pettigrew's half-imagined problems were releasing some very primitive feelings in her, she thought wryly. "I've left a schedule of events there on the desk, beside the phone, and a map. Everyone will get one tomorrow, but I thought you might like to familiarize yourself with the campus ahead of time."

"Yes. Thank you. Good-bye, Mr. Pettigrew. I'll see you tomorrow night." She shut the door firmly behind him and shook her head. Mr. Pettigrew was likely to be harder to handle than the fabled Mr. O'Brien.

She turned and began to open her suitcase. First, a nice cold shower, then a little nap on that inviting bed, and then, maybe, she would consider having a look at the campus. Since she hadn't been sure how long a time she'd be spending with Mr. Pettigrew, she had not planned for Harriet to arrive until after dinner.

That, too, had been a good idea, Fran thought as she took off her powder blue jacket and hung it in the closet. The cool air in the room felt delightful on her bare skin, but it did not make her consider the prospect of going outside again with much enthusiasm.

Still, just getting her clothes off, and getting away from the energy-draining Mr. Pettigrew had already made her feel better. She headed for the tiny shower.

Five minutes later, luxuriating under the lukewarm water, she thought she heard the ringing of the phone. Habit brought her out to answer it, and it wasn't until she stood beside it, dripping onto the floor, that she even thought of letting it go on ringing. She dismissed the thought. No doubt it was Harriet, impatient to know if she'd arrived.

"Hello, Harriet."

"Hello." The deep voice on the other end of the line was definitely not Harriet's. "Is this Fran Warren?"

"Yes." For some reason, Fran clutched the scanty towel tighter. "Who is this?"

His chuckle was warm and amused. "It's not Harriet, I'm afraid."

"I know that." She caught an irritable note in her voice and chalked it up to fatigue. "I would like to know who you are and what you want. I've been on an airplane all day and..."

"Caught you in the shower, did I?"

Suddenly Mr. Pettigrew's words came back to her. "This is Martin O'Brien, I suppose. All right, Mr. O'Brien, what can I do for you?"

"Did Petty tell you about the interview deal?"

She swallowed to contain her sudden laughter. His nickname for the conference director was devastatingly accurate. "Mr. Pettigrew told me that I would be doing a TV interview with you," she said crisply.

"Yeah, I bet he told you a lot of stuff about me."

Fran remained diplomatically silent. After all, the idea was to get *good* publicity for the conference and her book.

"Well, never mind that. I'd like to take you to lunch tomorrow. Have some time to talk. Get a feel for your book. The usual kind of thing."

A little shiver ran down Fran's back and she frowned thoughtfully. She was usually quite impervious to the obvious kind of charm that O'Brien exuded.

"That should be all right," she said a little stiffly. "Where shall I meet you?"

"Oh, I'll pick you up," O'Brien said. "Petty told me which dorm you'd be in. I'll come around twelve. Okay?"

"Okay. See you then."

As she put the receiver back in its cradle, another shiver ran over Fran's body. It was just that she found it embarrassing to be talking to a man even on the phone while she was clad only in a bath towel. She was tired, too, from her long flight. But neither of these rationalizations, as some part of her mind knew very well, really accounted for her body's strange reaction to the sound of Martin O'Brien's voice.

Chapter Two

Several hours later, having finished her shower and feeling much refreshed after pampering herself with a short nap, Fran was able to shove the charming Mr. O'Brien to the back of her mind and greet Harriet with a smile.

"Fran! Fran, darling!" Harriet had lost none of her college exuberance, Fran noted as she swept into the room. "It's so good to see you."

Fran was briefly enveloped in a cloud of perfume as Harriet hugged her and held her back to look at her more closely.

"Well," she pronounced, "you're looking fabulous!" Harriet touched a hand to her own perfectly coiffed hair. "So few women our age have kept their looks."

Fran laughed. "Harriet, you scoundrel. You make us sound ancient."

Harriet frowned, but even that couldn't make her look very serious. "Don't laugh, Fran Warren. We're going to be thirty this year, both of us. You know what a traumatic event that will be."

"*Can* be," Fran corrected with a smile. "You know, Harriet, problems like that originate in our heads. But, come on, sit down."

Harriet sighed dramatically as she put down her suitcase. "I hope you aren't going to play shrink all weekend," she said plaintively. "I have my own analyst, a brilliant woman, but very demanding. She's supposed to help me get my head on straight." Harriet grinned. "So hubby number three can be for keeps."

In spite of her friend's happy-go-lucky tone, Fran sensed the underlying pain. She attempted a laugh as she replied. "At least you've *had* a husband. Look at me."

"I do," Harriet said with obvious admiration. "As I said before, you look absolutely terrific." Harriet's innate good spirits came to the surface again. "While I"—she grimaced as she looked down at her fashionably clothed self—"I look like a frump."

Laughter spilled from Fran. If there was one thing Harriet was not and never had been, it was a frump. The years, and her husbands, had given her a certain level of sophistication, but she had always kept herself in shape.

Harriet laughed, too. "Well, I don't suppose I look that bad, but seriously, Fran, I want to talk to you about your theories." This time her sigh was quite real. "Dr. Hopkins thinks I've been afraid to try again. I haven't been too successful, you know."

"Everyone makes mistakes," Fran pointed out.

Harriet's laughter was tinged with sadness. "Yes, I suppose so. But there seem to be a lot of happily married people out there. I want that happiness, Fran. It's all I've ever really wanted—to have a good marriage and a good husband." She jumped to her feet and whirled away suddenly. "I want to celebrate a golden wedding anniversary!" she wailed.

"Harriet, my dear..." Fran kept her tone light, knowing that this was what her friend needed. "You're only twenty-nine years old. You may still do that."

Harriet threw herself into a chair. "I know, but sometimes I get frantic. That's been the whole point of my life, you know—to find a good husband." She grimaced. "As Dr. Hopkins has helped me to discover, it's not the easiest goal to set for oneself."

"Why don't you change your goal?" Fran asked. "You could think about a career."

Harriet shook her head. "I know that women much older than me are going back to school, studying for new careers. I've thought hard about it. But, Fran, the truth is so clear to me. I don't want a career. Even the most glamorous job means nothing to me, compared to finding the right man. It's awful to want something so badly and not be able to get it. It hurts, Fran," she said simply.

"I know."

There was something in Fran's tone that made Harriet look at her closely. "You, too! But I thought you liked your career."

"I do," Fran replied. "But why do you think I went to the trouble of writing that book? There are thousands of women like us, women who want to be happily married. I wanted to help them. And me."

"I've got the book," Harriet said, considering one perfectly manicured nail. "I've read it several times, too. I've been hoping maybe you'd give me some extra pointers."

"I'll be glad to help all I can," Fran replied, "but everything I know is in the book. Have you got a prospect in mind?"

Harriet shook her head. "No, Dr. Hopkins gave me the go-ahead only this week. We've been waiting until I was more certain of the kind of man I want."

"That's very good," Fran said encouragingly. "Why don't you make a list of the qualities you want in a man? Then we can discuss it."

Harriet beamed. "Oh, Fran, thank you. You're such a good friend."

"I hope so," Fran replied. "Now, maybe you can help me."

"Anything!" Harriet cried. "I'll do anything."

"Help me decide what to wear to lunch tomorrow with Martin O'Brien."

"You're lunching with the great Mr. O'Brien?"

Fran nodded.

"We call him the Memphis Heartthrob," Harriet confessed. "He's so attractive, no woman can resist him."

Fran's smile was grim. "This woman can. Mr. O'Brien has met his match. I'm up to here with men who think they know everything."

Harriet laughed. "Who told you he was like that?"

"Petty... Oh, no!" Fran clapped her hand over her mouth. "I mean, Mr. Pettigrew. Harriet, please, for heaven's sake, don't ever call him that."

"The name really fits, huh?" Harriet's eyes were filled with laughter.

Fran shrugged. "Sort of, but that's no excuse for using it. See? O'Brien's corrupted me already."

Harriet grinned. "That man can corrupt me any day of the week."

Fran shook her head. "I know he belongs on the list of no-win possibilities. But I'm not sure yet in which category."

"He's probably a love-'em-and-leave-'em type," Harriet said. "Otherwise, how could he still be single? But wait until you see him, Fran. He's absolutely delicious. He's tall, of course."

"Of course."

"And he's dark and handsome with the most dashing mustache and those wonderful eyes. Remember when we watched those old silent movies at school, and Valentino looked into the camera and your bones just seemed to melt?"

Fran laughed. "How could I forget? You practically swooned away."

Harriet sighed. "Of course. Well, anyway, O'Brien has eyes like that. Deep, dark brown. They make you want to..." Harriet shook herself. "He's really got charisma, my dear."

Fran shrugged. "And plenty of machismo to go with it, from the sound of things."

Harriet sighed again. "I suppose so. But as my grandmother used to say, he can put his slippers under my bed any day."

"Your grandmother?" Fran repeated. "That sweet little old lady with the snow-white hair?"

"The very same." Harriet grinned. "As she also used to say, she wasn't *always* a little old lady."

Again Fran had to laugh. "Our getting together was a great idea, Harriet," she said. "You always make me feel good." She glanced at her watch. "Are you tired?"

"What from?" Harriet inquired. "All I did was drive across town."

"Well, then, how about coming with me for a walk around the campus? I want to locate the various buildings so I'll be oriented on Monday, when classes begin."

"Sure," Harriet replied. "Just let me change." She glanced down at her fashionable pumps and her white silk dress. "These things are not made for hiking over college campuses." She headed toward the bathroom. "Be ready in a minute."

At noon the next day as Fran awaited the arrival of Martin O'Brien, she tried to calm herself by looking over the campus map. She and Harriet had walked for some time last night, gone to have a light meal, and sat up until the early hours of the morning laughing over their college escapades.

"Harriet," she called. "Come out of that bathroom and give me some moral support. You've been in there for hours."

"Coming." The Harriet that appeared looked like she'd stepped out of a fashion magazine. "Do I look all right?" she asked, turning slowly.

"You look marvelous," Fran replied, "as you very well know. I didn't know you had a date for lunch."

"I don't. But since O'Brien is coming here...well, Fran, the book does say not to pass up any opportunities. And he *is* single and available."

Fran laughed, ignoring an uncomfortable feeling in the pit of her stomach. "I guess you did read the book."

"Read it?" Harriet replied. "I practically memorized every word."

Fran managed to smile. "Well, then, sit down and talk to me until the great man arrives. You're supposed to be at ease, you know. Never let him know you're nervous."

For the thousandth time Fran wished that advice was as easy to follow as it was to give. She badly needed to feel at ease herself. For she was remembering with more and more clarity the strange and unnerving sensations that O'Brien's voice had raised in her. Now she was going to see the man in person, to have lunch with him. And from what Petty—Mr. Pettigrew—had said, she would need to have all her wits about her.

"What makes you think the great Mr. O'Brien..."

"Harriet!" Fran was shocked at her own sharpness. "Will you please stop talking as if the man were some kind of Greek god?"

Harriet just grinned. "What's the matter, Fran? Is this guy getting to you already?"

Fran frowned. "No, he's not. I'm just sick and tired of hearing about him. And to tell you the truth, Harriet, I'm rather off men at the moment."

Harriet stared. "Off men? Whatever for?"

"Well, there's the little matter of the no-win list. You do remember it?"

"Of course I do. The men to stay away from."

"Right. Well, I seem to be continually running into them. You wouldn't believe the kind of men they have doing local TV shows. I'm sick and tired of being laughed at, patronized, and treated as though my book is something I dreamed up for fun. I put a lot of hard scientific research into that book, including all the latest findings about human personality traits and relationships. And then some pompous old goat laughs at me or some ridiculous young one treats me like somebody's grandmother."

Harriet simply stared. "My goodness, Fran. I had no idea."

Fran threw up her hands. "Sorry, Harriet. I let myself get carried away."

A sharp rap on the door startled them both, and Fran's heart leaped up into her throat. "Just a minute," she called. Then, taking a deep breath, she slowly got to her feet. For a moment she regretted not getting more dressed up. Beside Harriet's sophisticated outfit, her simple blue cotton dress and low-heeled sandals looked very understated. But, she reminded herself, she was dressing for comfort in the Memphis heat, not for Martin O'Brien.

After getting a firm grip on herself, she opened the door. He was everything Mr. Pettigrew had said, and more. He was at least six feet tall, and there wasn't an extra ounce of fat on his body. He was dressed in cream-colored slacks and a sport shirt and his fabled brown eyes looked down into hers intently.

"I'm looking for Miss Warren," he said, his voice even deeper in person than on the phone. "But it looks like I've got the wrong room."

"No, Mr. O'Brien." She wished her voice would come out more boldly. It sounded too soft. "You have the right room. I'm Fran Warren."

"You?" The generous mouth under the dark mustache curved into a smile as his eyes moved over her. "I thought you were a college student. You look so young."

His technique is almost perfect, said the analytical part of her mind. And his looks… She cut the thought off.

"Won't you come in while I get my wrap?" she said, forcing a smile. "Sometimes the air conditioning down here is too cold for my northern bones."

"Very nice bones, too," he observed quietly as she stood aside to let him pass. To her annoyance she found her cheeks growing warm.

As he followed her into the room, Harriet looked up from the magazine she was pretending to read. She's too obvious, Fran thought; her need shows.

"This is my friend, Harriet Singleton," Fran said. "We're old college chums."

His perceptive eyes traveled over Harriet and then he smiled.

"I'm pleased to meet you, Mr. O'Brien," Harriet said with just a little too much eagerness.

"You must watch my show," O'Brien replied in a tone that made Fran want to kick him in the shins.

"Oh, no," she said quickly, sending Harriet a warning glance. "I just mentioned to Harriet that we were going to lunch to discuss the interview. I'm afraid she's far too busy socially to watch much TV. Aren't you, Harriet?"

Harriet nodded. "Oh, yes." But her words were overshadowed by the admiring way she looked at O'Brien.

Fran suppressed a rush of anger. It was unfair that a man should be able to make a woman act like a fool. "If you don't mind, Mr. O'Brien," she said pointedly, "perhaps we could get going."

"Of course. It was nice meeting you, Harriet," he said in a tone Fran thought far too condescending.

"Yes." Harriet nodded, still staring at him with obvious admiration.

From behind the man, Fran shook her head and glared at her friend. Harriet finally got the message. "See you later, Fran. Have a nice time." She turned back to her magazine.

O'Brien said no more; he simply followed Fran out the door. Once in the hall she felt a little better. Harriet's behavior left a bad taste in her mouth. No wonder O'Brien had such an ego, if females were always fawning over him.

Martin O'Brien's hand closed over her elbow and she jumped, startled as much by the tremor of shock that rushed through her body as by the unexpectedness of the touch.

O'Brien stopped walking and looked down at her with those deep, dark eyes. "Sorry," he said. "I didn't mean to startle you."

Only just in time did she remember Petty's fears of adverse publicity. If this interview hadn't been so important to him, she'd have been sorely tempted to turn on her heel and flee to the safety of her room.

Flee. The word echoed strangely in her mind. Fran Warren didn't flee from anything. Or anyone.

The second tempting thought was to remove her elbow from O'Brien's clasp and tell him in no uncertain terms that she was quite capable of walking without his assistance. But that temptation was better resisted, too, for the sake of Mr. Pettigrew's beloved conference. Anyway, a man like O'Brien might well take such a reaction as a challenge. And the very last thing she needed in an already complicated life was to have a man like O'Brien after her.

He was still looking down at her and she shook her head. "It's all right. I was just thinking of something else."

His eyes regarded her curiously and she moved off again. "Where are we going for lunch?" she asked, trying to distract her mind from several unpleasant thoughts concerning the fabulous Mr. O'Brien.

"I thought you might enjoy a place down on the river," he replied. "Do you like seafood?"

"Yes." He appears to be courteous, she thought cautiously and he *is* charming. There's certainly no doubt about that.

By this time they had reached the door to the street, and the hot, humid air engulfed her. Her steps slowed and she took several short breaths.

Beside her the big man chuckled. "Memphis in July can be a little much," he remarked. "You'll get used to it, though. I see you had the sense to dress for it."

"I'm afraid that comfort is more important to me than fashion," Fran said, trying to make her tone friendly.

He nodded seriously, "A very sensible attitude. You'd make a good Memphian."

This seemed like a reasonably safe topic and Fran resumed it after they had settled into the comfort of his air-conditioned car. "What makes a good Memphian?" she asked.

He sent her a casual glance before he eased the car into the stream of traffic. "Common sense," he said softly. "A little fortitude, though air conditioning has mostly eliminated the need for that. I guess you just have to love the place—or someone in it."

His tone had turned very serious, and though he smiled, it seemed forced. "Actually, summer is our worst season. Spring and fall are almost like summer up north, and winter is a real delight."

Fran considered asking him why he stayed in Memphis, but then decided against it. Martin O'Brien seemed like the sort of man who would not like talking about himself.

"Over there," he continued conversationally, "is the Pink Palace Museum, a local landmark. It was originally built as a home for Lawrence Saunders, the founder of the Piggly Wiggly Stores, but he went bankrupt before he could move in. Our most famous building is probably the Peabody Hotel where the big party for the conference is being held later in the week. It was the scene of some huge parties during the roaring twenties."

Fran looked dutifully wherever the man pointed, but her mind was not on what she saw. She was too busy trying to control the feelings rushing through her. Even though she knew that they were caused by chemistry and nothing more, it didn't seem to matter. Her body no longer cared that she was supposed to be an expert on keeping away from the wrong man, or that she didn't even like Martin O'Brien.

The restaurant was small and dark, more appropriate for an intimate rendezvous than a business lunch. But maybe this was O'Brien's style, Fran thought. This cozy atmosphere might help his guests to open up.

"Now," he said after they had ordered, "tell me about your book."

There was nothing offensive about his tone, yet she felt immediately on the defensive. "It addresses itself," she said in an academic tone, "to one of the biggest problems facing a woman."

"How to find a husband?" he suggested.

"Yes. For many women finding the right man is the main goal of their lives."

"I should think that would be relatively easy," he said. "People are getting married all the time."

"And divorced," she replied. "Divorce leaves a woman with a feeling of failure."

"A man, too, I imagine," he said pensively.

"A man, too," she agreed. "But a man's concerns are different. This book is for women."

"Unless a man wants to be forewarned. So he won't get 'caught.'"

Fran glared at him. "I didn't give the book that title," she explained. "And I don't like it. It makes the whole thing sound too..."

"Devious?" he suggested.

"No." Her reaction was immediate. "There's nothing devious about it. We naturally attract or repel people all the time. I just show women how to go about it consciously."

"In other words, you show them how to practice their wiles on men."

His tone was growing more and more provocative and her temper flared. "No, Mr. O'Brien, not how to practice their wiles. How to use proven scientific discoveries to get what they want."

"Sounds like the same thing to me," he said. "The same old lies and tricks. Butter up the poor sucker and reel him in, if you'll excuse my mixed metaphor. *How To Catch a Husband*." He made the words sound disgusting.

"Mr. O'Brien, what a sexist attitude!"

O'Brien shrugged. "It has nothing to do with sex. I'm against any kind of exploitation. If somebody wrote a similar book for men, I'd question it, too. Manipulation is always wrong; it doesn't matter who's doing it."

For some reason she believed him. "Have you read my book?" she asked. "It's not about manipulation."

The charming smile had faded by now and his tone turned frosty. "Oh yes, Miss Warren, I think it is. I read it. I read about every last, sly, little trick."

"Sly!" She was going to blow soon, she knew it. "There's nothing sly or tricky about my techniques. They're all based on the latest scientific discoveries about the human personality and male–female relationships."

O'Brien shook his head. "I don't like it. It isn't natural, it's manipulative. You should just let nature take its course."

Fran frowned. "That's exactly how we end up with so many divorces—by letting nature take its course."

Their salads arrived and she attacked hers with knife and fork, wishing she could stab the irritating Mr. O'Brien instead.

"What prompted you to write such a book?" O'Brien asked some minutes later as he pushed aside his empty salad plate.

"The need for it," she replied promptly.

"There are similar books on the market," he pointed out.

"When I began my work, there was nothing out that was scientifically grounded. I'm a practicing psychologist, Mr. O'Brien. I see people in trouble every day. I wanted to help them.''

"To catch a husband," he repeated, in that irritating tone.

"The publisher chose that title," Fran said, trying to stay calm. "He wanted something that would grab people. But just because a book has a commercial title doesn't mean it isn't sound. The original manuscript was full of footnotes.''

"I suppose the publisher took them out."

"That's right, Mr. O'Brien. So I settled for less than what I wanted, but I got the book published, and I got it out there where people could find it and be helped.''

"And you found some healthy royalty checks in your mail, no doubt.''

"'The workman is worthy of his hire,'" she quoted to him. "People in the service professions have to have food, shelter, and clothing just like everyone else." She eyed him quizzically. "I suppose you receive wages for your work. Very few of us are independently wealthy.''

He shrugged and she wondered if he knew that his movement called attention to the width of his shoulders. To her annoyance she also noticed several wisps of dark chest hair curling out of the open neck of his sport shirt. Another macho man, she thought with disgust. But her body reacted to him on a purely physical level, and she realized with a sense of shock that she would like to touch that chest where his shirt was open.

The whole thing was stupid, she told herself angrily. She had no respect or admiration for a man who made his living by harassing people. This attraction she had to him was only physical. She had never indulged herself in that kind of thing and she never would.

Their main course arrived while she was considering this and she tried to shift her thoughts to food. She was going to be in Memphis for only two weeks; surely she could handle things for that length of time. After that, the great Mr. O'Brien would become merely another figure in her past.

"I'd like to know something about the structure of the interview," she said between bites of steak.

"It's very simple. I ask the questions; you answer them."

"I see," she replied grimly. "And is this live or edited?"

"The interview is live," he answered sounding smug. "That adds to the excitement. But we usually have some video tape of the person at work." His smile was all charm, but his tone made her grit her teeth. "Since we can't tape you at your work on your masterpiece, I'll settle for some footage of you in the classroom."

"Mr. O'Brien, I came here to teach a class, not to do a TV show for you."

"We won't interfere," he said, calmly chewing his steak. "You just go ahead and do your thing."

Fran shook her head. "I'm surprised at you, Mr. O'Brien."

"Couldn't you make it Martin?" he asked, his brown eyes growing warmer.

"No. As I was about to say, Mr. O'Brien, don't you know that the observer always influences the experiment? There is no way that you could film my class without changing it."

"I'm aware of that theory," he said quietly, "just as I'm aware that people once held the belief that the world was flat. I don't give much credence to scientific theory, I guess—or to anything else that's establishment. In fact"—he grinned devilishly, the fabled eyes sparkling with amusement—"my chief pleasure in life is questioning cherished theories and beliefs."

"A strange pleasure," she commented. "One that grows from another's embarrassment."

He shrugged again. "The world, in case you haven't noticed lately, is definitely not a nice place. People need someone to defend them from the charlatans and con artists who are always infringing on them." His eyes met and held hers and she shivered. "Besides, having his ideas challenged helps a person know what he believes."

She was aware of the truth of this statement, but she continued. "I don't see why that gives you the right to rip into people."

His smile was lazy and provocative, and extremely irritating. "Why, Miss Warren, you shouldn't believe everything you hear. Petty is about as far from your objective observer as it's possible to get."

That, she thought, could hardly be denied. "Nevertheless, Mr. O'Brien, I think your approach is all wrong."

He smiled again. "I get it. You favor the old, 'you can catch more flies with honey than vinegar' approach. I'm afraid I just don't agree with that. I think people ought to be willing to stand up for their convictions. Stand up and be counted.''

Chapter Three

Stand up and be counted. The next morning while getting ready for class, it was those words that Fran remembered most. She had to admit that there was a certain sense to O'Brien's contention that a person should be willing to stand up for himself. Many times in the past, she had quite willingly defended her beliefs. Certainly, O'Brien was not the first man to attack her book or to try to put down her work, but he was the first to have affected her like this. It was hard to concentrate on logic and rebuttal when his eyes lingered on her in that strangely personal way. It was like dealing with two different people. And she had to admit to herself that if O'Brien had been in any other profession she might just have used some of her well-researched methods on *him*.

She shook her head stubbornly and turned away from the mirror. Mr. O'Brien might interfere with her class, especially on the first day, but she was certainly not going to make matters any worse by reacting irrationally.

Picking up her books, she turned toward the bathroom and said, "Harriet, come on. It's time to go."

"You go on, Fran." Harriet's voice was muffled by the bathroom door. "I've botched my left eye and have to do it over. I'll see you there."

"Okay." Fran didn't bother to argue. She knew from experience that nothing could persuade Harriet to leave the bathroom until she was completely satisfied with her appearance.

Fran looked down at her own casual outfit as she left the dorm room. She was wearing the same dress and sandals that she'd worn to lunch the day before. Her sun-bleached hair hung loose on her shoulders and her make-up was minimal. She was determined to behave just as she would have if Martin O'Brien had never existed.

Despite the earliness of the hour, the heat was oppressive. The hot air seemed wet and heavy in her lungs, but after a moment its effects faded from her consciousness. Her whole mind was focused on the upcoming class. If O'Brien ruined it...

Fran found her free hand clenching into a fist, and she slowly opened it, willing herself to relax. She would do the best she could, and the uppity Mr. O'Brien could just go...

I'm a professional, she told herself as she neared the classroom. I will be calm, cool, and collected.

The room was small. Three or four people were already there with notebooks open to clean white pages. "Good morning," Fran said and received a chorus of replies. She put her books on the table and considered the room, with its chairs arranged in the usual stiff rows.

"Well," she said aloud, "the first thing to do is to get these chairs into a circle." Soon everyone was pushing chairs around.

"Thank you," said Fran, when they were seated. "That's much better."

By this time the room held fifteen students, ranging from several with white hair to a pair of jean-clad teen-aged boys. "My name is Fran Warren," she said, scooping her books off the table and taking one of the chairs. "And I'm here to help you write a how-to book." She smiled and the faces around the circle smiled back. "Now," she said, warming to the class and almost forgetting that O'Brien would be arriving any moment, "the first thing I want to do..."

The noise at the door could have been another student, but she knew instinctively that it was not.

"Good morning," Martin O'Brien said cheerfully. "We're ready to roll."

Fran took a deep breath and reminded herself: be calm, cool, and collected. "Mr. O'Brien will be filming some portions of the class for a show later this week." A rustle of excitement swept over the students and Fran cursed silently. Now she would have trouble holding their attention.

"Don't mind us." O'Brien spoke to the class, but as his eyes met Fran's she knew his amusement was for her.

She stiffened her back. "As much as possible, I would appreciate your ignoring the camera. We have a lot of territory to cover. Now, first of all..."

The door opened to admit Harriet, and Fran bit back a sharp comment. If only Harriet was as concerned about being on time as she was about her appearance. As Fran motioned her to an empty chair, the camera swung around to record her entrance.

Fran waited until the room was quiet again. "Now," she said for the third time, "I'd like to begin by getting to know a little about you. So let's go around the circle. Tell us your name, your reason for being in this class, and what kind of how-to book you're interested in writing."

The man on her left went first. "My name is Harold Wilson," he said. "I'm a retired banker. But my hobby's always been roses, and I want to write a book about starting a rose garden."

As the people sitting around the circle introduced themselves, Fran tried to forget the camera that was recording everything. Harder to ignore was the fact that O'Brien had taken a seat on her right and was clearly enjoying himself.

The replies were rather run-of-the-mill; members of the class were contemplating books about such diverse subjects as making pies with the flakiest crust and buying the best motor bike.

Everything seemed to be going well, until Harriet's turn. "I'm Harriet Singleton," she said, smiling sweetly at the camera, "and I'm looking for the perfect husband."

The class exploded into laughter, but Harriet appeared not to mind. "Fran—Miss Warren—and I went to school together. I'm studying her book."

Thankfully, the camera moved on and Fran managed to swallow her anger. O'Brien's presence was making a charade of her getting-acquainted session, and there was not a thing she could do about it without getting bad publicity for Mr. Pettigrew's precious conference.

Finally, the camera reached O'Brien himself. "Martin O'Brien here," he said. "I want to see what makes Miss Warren tick."

Aware that the camera was now trained on her, Fran addressed the class. "Thank you all for sharing with us. Now, I like a very informal class structure. If a question comes to mind while I'm talking, ask it then. Questioning is one of the best ways of learning, and to be most effective, the questions should be asked when they first occur to you. Do you understand?"

Heads nodded.

"Miss Warren?" One of the teen-aged boys raised a hand.

"Yes, Don?"

"Are we going to be on TV?"

Fran swallowed a sigh. What she would like to do to Martin O'Brien! "I'm afraid that's up to Mr. O'Brien." She turned to him.

"I can't promise," O'Brien said. "But the way it looks now, I'll probably use the whole sequence."

"When will it be on?" asked the other teen-ager, obviously excited by the chance to be on television.

"Thursday, at my usual time," O'Brien said. "I'll be interviewing Miss Warren live."

As the eyes of everyone swung back to her, Fran was aware of an urge to scream. The first day of class was always difficult but this... She took a firm grip on her temper, reminding herself again: be calm, cool, and collected. "Now," she continued, "the first thing you must have to write a book is motivation. All those words don't jump onto the page by themselves." She resisted an urge to look at O'Brien, who was thankfully out of her direct line of vision.

"Books, at least non-fiction ones," she continued, "must have some information to relay. If you're going to write a how-to book, you must really know your subject. And it must be a subject that is important to you."

"Like the subject of your book," O'Brien interjected in a cheerful voice. "Tell us, Miss Warren, why you chose the subject you did."

There was no point in trying to evade his questions since he would only pursue them that much harder. The thing to do was to answer his question while making a point for the class.

"I chose my subject," she said, "for several reasons. First, as a practicing psychologist, I saw many women who were leading sad and lonely lives because they could not find the right husbands. Thus, I knew that there were readers out there who would be interested in my book. Second, in my efforts to help my clients, I had done a great deal of research into the subject of human relationships. This is the other prerequisite for a how-to book. First, an interested audience. Second, some important knowledge to impart to them."

"How scientific are the precepts in your book?" O'Brien asked with that nasty look in his eyes.

"It is as scientific as I could make it," Fran replied, automatically resisting a desire to tell this irritating man off, camera or no camera. "I considered all the work I could find on the development of relationships."

"Wouldn't it have been just as easy," O'Brien said, "to run over the old list of tricks? Women have been using their wiles to catch husbands for hundreds of years now. Why bother to put a scientific gloss on the thing?"

This time his tone of attack was clearly evident. Stay calm, Fran told herself.

"My book is based on scientific fact; it's not a glossing over of old tricks." She wrinkled her nose distastefully. "I think perhaps you would find some research in this area helpful, Mr. O'Brien. Reactions between people occur, whether they are conscious of them or not. Since this is true, a person might as well be conscious of what's going on."

O'Brien shrugged. "Maybe. But I have to admit that I resent a book that's supposed to show women how to catch husbands."

He smiled at the class, clearly inviting them to support his view. "It doesn't seem fair to me. Some poor sucker is just sitting there, minding his own business, and along comes this woman who decides to hook him. The guy doesn't even know what hit him. One minute he's free and happy, the next he finds himself on the way to the altar."

"Mr. O'Brien," Fran protested, "you are exaggerating terribly. A man who doesn't want to be married would hardly be influenced by the techniques offered in the book. There has to be something there to build on. And contrary to your opinion, there are also men out there looking for love and marriage. Not everyone prefers a single existence."

"You seem to." The words were quietly spoken, but they sent a wave of shock through her already tense body, and several members of the class gasped audibly at such effrontery.

"I believe in marriage," Fran said coolly. "As difficult as it can be to share one's life with another person, I believe the effort is worthwhile." She turned and faced O'Brien squarely. "I also believe that such an important relationship should be considered very carefully. For a marriage to work, one must have the right sort of partner." She paused, her eyes traveling around the circle. "I've seen what havoc can be caused when people make the wrong choices. So, it's really very simple, Mr. O'Brien. I just haven't found the right man yet."

"But when you do, you'll practice synchronization tricks on him," O'Brien replied. "You'll breathe in the same rhythms as he does, sit the way he does, talk as softly or as loudly as he does."

"Those are not tricks," Fran explained patiently, conscious of the avid interest of the class. "Research has shown that these are the ways people in love naturally respond to teach other. They unconsciously synchronize their gestures, their breathing, their steps, their tone of voice, and even, eventually, their heartbeats. I'm sure you must be aware that one can acquire certain characteristics by acting as though she or he already has them. Thus, impatient people can become patient by acting that way, and timid people can become assertive in the same fashion."

O'Brien had not lost any of his poised cheerfulness, and she wondered briefly how the man could look so relaxed and ask such pointed questions. "I still say it isn't natural. These things should be left alone just to happen."

Fran shook her head and looked around the circle of expectant faces. "That, Mr. O'Brien, is an absurd argument. I presume you visit the doctor and the dentist. You drive a car, wear clothes made of synthetics, and eat frozen foods. You seem quite willing to take advantage of scientific research in all the other areas of your life." She took a deep breath. "It so happens that for many women a relationship is the only legitimate reason for being. To deny them the latest discoveries is to hamper them in their search for happiness." As her eyes swept around the circle, several heads nodded, including Harriet's carefully coiffed one.

"That's right," said a silver-haired woman. "Things have always favored the men. They do the asking. But a woman has to have some chance of getting what she wants. She has to be able to do something."

"Girls who run after guys turn me off," said Don, the teen-ager who wanted to write about buying a motor bike. His grin grew wider and he glanced at O'Brien. "But I've got to admit, if it was the right chick and she did it sort of easy-like...well, that wouldn't be too hard to take."

Mr. Wilson shook his head. "Women are so aggressive these days, I can hardly believe it. I'm a widower and have been for several years. Every time I go over to the senior center the women are after me." For a moment, his grin made him look years younger. "But I guess maybe I've got to agree with the young man." His smile turned wistful. "My Emma was the sweetest thing, but now that I think of it, she gave me more than one little nudge."

"But don't you see?" O'Brien pointed out. "It's the subtlety that makes it wrong. Things should be aboveboard and direct between people."

"Young man, you are wrong," said Mrs. Parker, the elderly woman who now entered the conversation. Her eyes sparkled dangerously as she confronted O'Brien. "Of course women have marriage on their minds. How can they help it when it's always being pounded into their heads? But they can hardly approach a strange man and say, 'Let's get married.'" She regarded him shrewdly. "I hate to say it about such a nice-looking young man, but you're just not making sense. The way you questioned Miss Warren about her personal life, I'm beginning to wonder if there's something in *your* past that makes you take such an unreasonable attitude.''

For the first time since she'd met him, Fran saw Martin O'Brien look uncomfortable. Pain registered on his handsome face and he reminded Fran of a wounded animal. It looked like Mrs. Parker had hit very close to home.

"Well," Fran said, drawing the attention away from him, "that's enough about my book. We're here to discuss writing how-to books, not personal relationships. So let's get down to work."

Out of the corner of her eye, she saw O'Brien staring at her. He was probably wondering why she had rushed in to save him from embarrassment. She was wondering the same thing herself. Given his condescending attitude toward her and her work, she should have jumped to join the attack, not deflect it.

But then, she had never been an aggressive person. Hers was a service profession and she had entered into it because she wanted to help people. The pain caused by Ashley's leaving her might have had something to do with her choice. But she had already decided on her profession and had been in school for several years when Ashley discovered the cute little thing who swept him off his feet and caused him to break his engagement to her.

She understood very thoroughly what had happened and why. Love was not, after all, completely under one's control. And she was quite sure that particular bit of personal history had nothing whatever to do with her single state. It was just as she had told O'Brien: she had not yet found the right man. When she did, she would follow the methods outlined in her book.

All this had raced through her mind as her eyes made a circuit of the room. "Now, for the next session, I'd like you to do several things. First, try to come up with a title for your book." Her eyes avoided O'Brien's and the amusement she knew she would find there. "It should appeal to the kind of readers you want to attract. It can be catchy or informative, but it should never promise more than you can deliver."

She expected a reaction from O'Brien on that, but none came. "Next, I want a paragraph of purpose. This probably won't be included in the finished book, but will help you to focus on exactly what you want your book to say and do."

Again she looked around the circle, avoiding Martin O'Brien's eyes. "Okay. So you'll have a title and a paragraph of purpose. Then prepare a tentative table of contents. List the chapters with headings and note what each will be about. Tomorrow we'll begin discussing your work." Several people stirred uncomfortably and she smiled at them. "Don't worry about that. Listening to other people's reactions will help you to focus your own work." Her smile broadened. "I don't allow the members of my classes to attack each other's work."

"Or their ideas, I hope," Mrs. Parker said with a sidelong glance at O'Brien.

"Or their ideas," Fran echoed. "Although sometimes opposition is useful in helping us to discover what we believe." Now, why did I say that? she wondered.

Another woman, middle-aged and overweight, raised her hand timidly. "Are we going to be observed again tomorrow?" she asked plaintively. "I find the camera very distracting, and truthfully, I don't want to discuss my book in front of it."

"Yes," Mrs. Parker added. She was clearly going to do a lot of talking in this class. "I don't care for it, either." She glanced at O'Brien. "And I think if Mr. O'Brien plans to sit in on the class, he should do the assignments like the rest of us. That way his presence won't be so disruptive." Several heads nodded and the class turned to look at O'Brien.

"But I don't want to write a how-to book," he objected, though not too strenuously, Fran observed.

"I'm sure it would be very helpful to you," Mrs. Parker said softly, with that dangerous gleam in her eye.

"But I don't have a subject."

"You can write about doing TV interviews," the timid woman said, obviously pleased with an idea that would put O'Brien on the same level as everyone else.

He shrugged, still maintaining his cheerful pose. "Well, if that's what everyone wants..."

A chorus of yeses went up around the circle.

"And what about the camera?" the persistent Mrs. Parker asked. What a blessing that woman was! Fran thought. All of these remarks were much better coming from the class than from her.

"I was hoping to get some footage of Miss Warren teaching," O'Brien replied. "But how about a compromise? Charlie here"—he indicated the cameraman—"will only shoot Miss Warren and me occasionally. Unless, that is, some of you want to volunteer.''

Fran looked at her students. She would really like to get rid of the camera altogether, but she realized that O'Brien had a job to do. "Is that agreeable?" she asked. Heads nodded. "Good." She glanced at her watch. "Well, time's up for today. Bring your assignments with you tomorrow." She counted them off on her fingers. "Title, paragraph of purpose, and table of contents. I'll see you then."

She got to her feet, moving away from O'Brien. The less she had to do with the man, the better. She saw Harriet coming toward her, a frown on her face. But before she could get through the crowd, O'Brien had a hold on Fran's elbow. "Say, teach," he said as she swung around to face him. "How about dinner tonight?"

Carefully, she withdrew her elbow from his grasp. Her blood was racing and her body was extremely sensitive to the nearness of his. But, although her body had gone crazy, her mind remained clear. She knew that Martin O'Brien was nothing at all like the man she was looking for. He had strength, but it was the wrong type. He had character, but not the kind she could admire. And his good looks only made him more dangerous.

He looked down at her with those liquid brown eyes. "Sorry, Mr. O'Brien," she said in a tone that sounded more smug than regretful, "but I have a dinner engagement for this evening. Some other time, perhaps."

She heard Harriet's half-smothered gasp of surprise behind her, but she didn't turn. "Will you be in class tomorrow, Mr. O'Brien?"

His surprise at her refusal was instantly replaced by an irritatingly cheerful look. "Oh, I'll be here, Miss Warren, clutching my finished assignment."

She permitted herself a small, satisfied smile. "Very well, Mr. O'Brien, I'll see you then."

Chapter Four

A stern glance kept Harriet silent until the rest of the class had left the room. But the door had barely closed behind the last of them before she cried, "How could you?"

Although she knew perfectly well what Harriet was getting at, Fran delayed by gathering up her books and asking innocently, "How could I what?"

"How could you turn down a date with that fabulous man?" Harriet's manicured hands fluttered madly in the air. "You're not following your own advice. The book says to give a man a chance."

Fran shrugged. "Mr. O'Brien had his chance when I went to lunch with him. I'm sick and tired of having men like him take pot shots at me."

She looked outside. "Let's take our stuff back to the room and go get lunch. Then, maybe we'll go for a swim."

Harriet frowned. "I don't want to get my hair wet before the reception tonight. Larry did such a nice job on it."

Fran nodded. Harriet had always been overly anxious about her appearance, probably due to some insecurity about herself as a person. Fran simply washed her hair and let it dry naturally, something Harriet would never do.

As they moved down the corridor, Harriet sighed dramatically. "I could forgive a man like that a lot of things," she announced.

Fran frowned. "There are some things that can't be forgiven," she pointed out. "Or, at least, they shouldn't be."

Both of Harriet's husbands had fallen into the no-win category and were the kind of men Fran advised women to avoid. The first, considerably older than Harriet, had turned the bubbling, fun-loving girl into a sophisticated woman and then left her for another fun-loving girl. The second, much younger, had expected Harriet to provide him with a plush life, but soon got bored with it and her.

"Have you ever considered dressing more casually and doing your own hair?" Fran asked as they reached the outdoors and paused to let their lungs acclimate to the heavy air. What the heck, she might as well take a shot at it.

Just as she had expected, Harriet looked surprised. "No. Why should I? I can afford what I have."

"I wasn't thinking of that," Fran explained, picking her words with care. "It's just that...well, the way we look advertises the people we are. And I don't believe that inside you're all that sophisticated. Sometimes we attract the wrong people or don't attract the right ones, because we look like something we're not."

Harriet walked on silently for several minutes and Fran remained quiet, too. There was not much more she could say on the subject.

Finally, her friend spoke. "I'm sure you know what you're talking about," she said. "But I've been this way for a long time. I feel naked unless I'm dressed properly."

Fran swallowed a sigh. "That's just it, Harriet. Whose idea of proper dress are you conforming to? Yours or Pierre's?"

Again Harriet hesitated. "Pierre's, I suppose. But I've always liked to look nice."

"Yes, I know. Well, it's only an idea, so think about it. There is something else you'll have to do, though."

"What?"

"You're going to have to do the assignments. You heard what the class decided. I can't make an exception for you just because you're my friend."

Harriet sighed. "Life sure is complicated. This thing isn't working out at all the way I'd planned."

"How had you planned it?" Fran asked, as they neared their room.

"I thought we'd do a lot of talking and you'd give me tips on finding the right man."

Fran chuckled. "I thought that's what I *was* doing."

Harriet smiled sadly. "But I didn't bargain for making myself over...or for having to write a book. What can I write a book about?" Her smile faded. "How to lose a husband?"

"Come on, Harriet. Cut it out. Think about what you know."

"I don't know anything," Harriet almost wailed.

"That's not true. You know about fashion and makeup."

Harriet shook her head. "I don't know enough to do a book."

"You decorate a house with marvelous flair. You also give fabulous parties."

"That's it!" Harriet cried. "I do give great parties, and I always have. That's something that neither of my husbands taught me. That's part of the real me." She paused and stared at her friend. "That's it, isn't it, Fran? I have to find the real me before I can find the right man. That's what you were talking about with the clothes and the hair stuff."

Fran nodded. "Something like that. But that doesn't mean you have to forget about everything you've learned from someone else. It just means taking a personal inventory and deciding what you want to keep and what you don't. If you really like spending all that time on makeup and having your hair done every week, then go on doing it. But do it because *you* want to, not because someone else said you should." Fran shrugged. "Who am I to say? Maybe you enjoy it."

Harriet grimaced. "I don't," she said. "Not really. But Pierre made such a production of it, and Phillip was so young..." Harriet paused, unable to hide the pain. "I was always afraid of losing him. And of course, I did." She laughed bitterly. "Well, that's all water over the dam. Anyway, Fran, thanks for the talk. I'll be doing a lot of thinking about it; you can be sure of that."

That evening, when they set out for the reception, Fran wondered how much thinking her friend had done. Harriet's glossy black hair remained intricately styled and her long chic gown of maroon silk fit like a glove.

About one thing, Harriet had been right: they had both maintained their youthful figures. But, walking across campus in the simple cotton caftan she had brought for this occasion, Fran wished she had a more sophisticated gown. She had put on the blue beads and dangling blue earrings that she had been told matched her eyes, and ordinarily she would have thought she looked quite nice, but beside the dramatic Harriet she almost felt dowdy.

What would O'Brien think of these feelings of hers? Would he attribute them to jealousy? Would he also think that what she'd said to Harriet earlier about changing her image had been motivated by envious feelings? It hadn't been; she knew herself well enough to be aware of that. But, she realized as she continued to examine her motives, they had been selfish feelings.

She wanted the old Harriet back, the one who thought life was a wonderful, exciting adventure. Her unfortunate marriages, or the sophistication Pierre had insisted upon, had dimmed much of Harriet's enthusiasm. At any rate, Fran wanted her friend to re-capture that joy of living that had once made her so much fun. You're not exactly a ball of fire, she re-minded herself rather crossly. Try working on yourself.

"Hey, Harriet." She turned to her friend. "Re-member the junior prom?"

"Remember?" Harriet squealed. "How could I forget? I had the most beautiful rose-colored dress." She laughed. "I wanted red, but Mom said red wasn't appropriate for a prom, so we compromised on the rose. It had little straps, but I tucked them down once I got away from the house. And Hank Witherspoon brought me the biggest, purplest orchid! It clashed dreadfully with my gown, but I loved it. It was my first orchid, and my first long gown."

Fran nodded, watching Harriet's shining face. This was the friend she knew and loved.

"It was a marvelous evening." Harriet's laughter rang out. "Even when that stupid bug flew down the front of my dress." She turned glowing eyes to Fran. "That's the way I want to feel again, Fran. Like the world's out there, just waiting for me."

"It is, Harriet," Fran said gently. "The difference isn't in the world. It's still the same exciting place. The difference is in us."

"Well, then," Harriet said, her eyes gleaming, "let's make a pact. Starting tonight, life is an adven-ture again." She chuckled. "Do you suppose that lus-cious Mr. O'Brien will be at the reception?"

"I hope not." The moment the words left Fran's mouth she was aware that they were not true. Her mind might have put Mr. O'Brien in the no-win category, but her body had some very different and disquieting ideas. It had been a long time since she'd felt such a strong pull toward a man, and she was tempted to see if O'Brien was really interested in her. But he wasn't going to be at the reception anyway, she reminded herself. Such a function would hold no interest for him.

"Oh, look," Harriet cried as they entered the reception hall, with its low lights and tables filled with flowers. "It even reminds me of a prom."

Fran smiled at her friend. It was good to be with Harriet again. That, at least, had been a good idea.

"Miss Warren." Mr. Pettigrew came bustling across the room, his face screwed up in its usual worried expression. "There you are."

Fran nodded. There wasn't much point in saying anything, Mr. Pettigrew usually did all the talking.

"Come with me," he said. "I want you to meet the other writers. They're all over here."

"Mr. Pettigrew..." Fran began, noticing that Harriet was smiling broadly.

"You just go on, Fran," Harriet said. "I think I see someone I know over there."

Fran turned to look in the same direction, but she didn't see anyone she recognized. Then Petty had her by the arm and was dragging her across the floor.

By the time he had finished introducing her to the other writers, Harriet had disappeared into what was rapidly becoming a crowd.

"Old Petty," a male voice muttered from behind her, "leaves a lot to be desired as a conference director."

Her heart rose up in her throat, and beneath the caftan her knees began to quiver. She forced her voice to remain cool. "You, of course, have organized innumerable affairs and know all about arranging conferences."

Fran forced herself to turn and meet his eyes. His smile was warm and inviting, and she found herself holding her breath.

"I know enough to see that when the most desirable woman in the room isn't dancing, something's got to be wrong."

It took a moment for the outrageous compliment to register, since it came from Martin O'Brien. Then she deliberately chose to misunderstand it. "You mean Harriet is standing around somewhere? I should go find her."

"You'll do no such thing," O'Brien said firmly. "I wasn't talking about her, and you know it."

"Why, Mr. O'Brien..."

"I think, since we're going to be in close contact for the next several weeks, that you ought to call me Martin."

"Really, Mr. O'Brien. We're antagonists, practically enemies. I don't think first names are called for in light of the circumstances."

"I was only doing my job," he said, taking on the expression of a hurt little boy. "I don't hold your job against you."

"Your logic is faulty," she said. "I did not attack you."

"Sure you did," he replied cheerfully. "You attacked my interviewing methods. Come on, now, admit it."

She did have to admit that. "But only..." she began.

He stepped close and put his hand on her waist. For some insane reason she didn't pull away. "Tell you what," he said softly. "Let's call a truce for tonight. You forget that you're a shrink who wrote a provocative book, and I'll forget that I'm a mean TV interviewer with a big bad mouth."

She found herself laughing, her antagonism dissolving in the warmth of his smile. There was a lot of sense in what he said. The professional persona did not reveal the whole character. Behind that biting tongue there might well be a wonderful man.

Warning signs flashed in her mind, but she ignored them. The sensible life she'd been leading lately was dull and lonely. She craved some excitement and adventure.

His arm around her waist felt marvelous and she smiled up at him. "Agreed," she said. "A truce for tonight—with an additional stipulation."

He sighed. "I should have known."

"Anything that passes between us tonight is off the record."

His eyes gleamed. "You've got a deal," he said. "Now, Miss Warren, may I have the honor of this dance?"

"Yes, Martin," she said, enjoying his look of surprise. "And do call me Fran."

His arm slid around her waist, pulling her close. The effect was so overwhelming that she was afraid her feet would not move. But they automatically followed his, just as the curves of her body seemed to fit perfectly against him. She breathed in the smell of his after-shave, and the dark hair at his collar brushed her fingers as they lay on the shoulder of his suit.

"You dance well," he said, his lips so close to her ear that she could feel his warm breath.

"So do you." The words came out before she thought about them. Part of her mind told her she was acting like a silly schoolgirl. But she decided immediately that she really didn't care. She was going to have some fun and enjoy the feelings Martin O'Brien aroused in her rather than fighting them off.

"Do you dance much?" O'Brien asked softly.

His shoulder was only an inch away from her cheek and she longed to lay her face against it. "I used to," she said, turning her face toward his and finding it so close that she stumbled.

His arm steadied her and he gathered her closer, so that she had to turn away again. But even as she did, she kept the picture of those brown eyes in her mind. There was so much feeling shining in their depths. And his lips had been so close to hers. It had been a long time since she'd been kissed by a man with a mustache. How would it feel?

She saw the danger signs again, and heard the warnings of her mind. But they were all far away, barely penetrating the sweet, romantic fog in which she moved.

Tonight everything was perfect. Her body fit with precision into his arms and moved with certainty to his steps. There seemed no need for words; the physical harmony between them was complete. She couldn't ask for anything more. The temptation became too much for her and she let her cheek rest lightly against his shoulder.

The arm that held her drew her closer still, and his hand pulled hers inward, against his other shoulder. They moved in perfect rhythm with each other and the music.

His lips were almost touching her ear, and she could hear the gentle intake of his breath. Slowly she realized that her breathing matched his. Synchronization technique number two, she thought. She had automatically followed one of the rules of her book without consciously planning to. Abruptly, she let go of her analysis and faded back into the romantic moment.

It ended too quickly. As the music stopped, she saw Harriet's startled face over O'Brien's shoulder. A man stood by Harriet's side, but Fran didn't pay any attention. With a sigh she pulled herself back into reality. "I really should go speak to Harriet," she said.

"Your well-dressed friend? All right, I'll take you to her."

Seeing them move toward her, Harriet put on a smile. "Why, hello, Mr. O'Brien. I didn't think you'd be here."

"I, too, like to relax from time to time," O'Brien said. He turned slightly as he felt Fran stiffen beside him.

"Ashley?"

The man beside Harriet smiled. "The very same, Fran. How are you?"

"I'm fine," she replied automatically, struggling to regain her wits. "What are you doing here?"

"I wanted to talk to you," Ashley said. "But, come on, I'm dying to dance with you first."

Fran started to reply, but O'Brien had already turned to Harriet. "Mrs. Singleton?"

"I'd like that," Harriet said, a quiet smile of satisfaction on her face.

As she stepped into Ashley's arms, Fran made a mental note to ask Harriet if she had brought Ashley here. The last thing Fran wanted was to be involved again with the man who had brought her so much misery.

"Harriet tells me you've never married," Ashley said as he moved her around the dance floor. There was no denying he was a good dancer, but for some reason she could not match her steps to his. She felt awkward and angry, all her pleasant feelings gone.

"And how is Amy?" she asked, hoping her voice sounded calm.

"I don't know." Ashley gripped her tighter and she automatically resisted, pulling back against his arm. "She and I split up. She wasn't the right woman for me, Fran. I've always wanted you."

For a moment she was overpowered by memories, and the pain of his desertion. Then it passed and she realized with immense gratitude that she *was* truly finished with Ashley. "I'm very sorry to hear that," she said in a voice that she might have used with a client.

Ashley seemed startled. "I thought you'd be pleased."

It was Fran's turn to be startled. "Why on earth should I be pleased? Divorce is a terrible thing."

Ashley smiled smugly. "Because now you and I can get together again, like we should have years ago."

Fran stopped dancing abruptly and extricated herself from his arms. "I'm afraid you have the wrong idea, Ashley. I got over you years ago."

"But, Fran, baby..."

His use of the endearing term made her draw in her breath. How dare he think that he could come waltzing back into her life after all these years and find her waiting for him? But he wasn't worth getting angry over. "It's all over," she repeated firmly.

Spinning on her heel, she turned and ran into a broad masculine chest. "Easy," said O'Brien's deep voice. "Don't let the creep get to you."

His arm tightened around her and she fell against him again, all her anger dissipating, and her body rhythms soothed. Her feet moved easily in step with his. Synchronization technique number four: synchronize your steps. This was getting to be too much, she thought.

"What sent you crashing to my rescue?" she asked softly, her lips near his ear.

He turned to face her and again her heart pounded. "First, I didn't crash. I was actually very discreet. I wanted to punch his lights out." For some strange reason the ferocity in his voice warmed her heart. "But instead I thought of your needs first and I presented myself as your savior.''

She felt light-headed, almost giddy. "Well done, sir knight," she said. "Well done."

He smiled teasingly. "I imagine even the most altruistic of knights got their rewards."

"And what sort of reward does my knight want?" she asked lightly, enjoying the game.

"Holding you in my arms is reward enough," he said softly, but his eyes glistened dangerously. "For now, at least." He grinned. "I'd like to tell you that I sensed your need for me. But the truth is your friend Harriet told me about Ashley and how marvelous it is that now you and he can get together again. Personally, Ashley doesn't look like such a good bet to me." He pulled her closer. "And I figured a lady with your pride wouldn't be interested in a loser like that."

"What makes you think he's a loser?" she asked, wondering how she could feel so incredibly safe in this man's arms.

"He lost *you,*" O'Brien said firmly. "Come to think of it, I guess I ought to pity the poor guy. At least he seems to have realized what he lost. A little too late, though. But enough about old Ashley. Let's forget him and just enjoy ourselves. This is our night."

"Yes," she murmured, hiding her head against his shoulder. She wanted this one marvelous night. Surely she deserved that much. Tomorrow she and O'Brien would be antagonists again, in disagreement about practically everything. But tonight they were in perfect harmony, their bodies circling the dance floor together, their breathing synchronized.

This perfect feeling might be an illusion, brought on by Harriet's memories of their first prom, but no matter what had caused it, Fran was going to enjoy it for all it was worth.

Chapter Five

When Fran woke up the next morning, it took her a moment to remember where she was. She'd been dreaming, of course, and it took time to separate the dream from reality—especially since the dream had been a continuation of the previous evening. She sighed. In the bright light of the morning, last night suddenly seemed like a dream.

The part of the night where she had danced with Martin had been so romantic. She smiled wistfully. He might not be good husband material, but Martin O'Brien made a wonderful date. He said and did all the right things.

He had even helped her relax and forget about Ashley's ridiculous proposition. She let her mind wander back over the entire evening. It was good to know that Ashley meant nothing to her now. Of course, his behavior had been disturbing, especially since he had insisted on cutting in on her and Martin several times.

And Harriet... Fran moved restlessly. Harriet had tried to act more restrained, but she had still been too coy with Martin.

Fran sighed and rolled over in the narrow bed. Martin was no good for Harriet; anyone could see that. He was too self-assured and she was too insecure. Besides, Martin had seemed indifferent to Harriet's sophisticated charm. In fact, he hadn't seemed interested in anyone but Fran.

A small shiver ran through Fran's body. They had danced together the whole night, holding to their truce. They had not spoken much, yet they had been in perfect communication.

During the last dance, when the lights had been lowered, he'd danced her into a secluded corner and kissed her. Her heart had pounded so madly she was sure he must have felt it. His lips had been soft and warm, his mustache only a tickle on her upper lip. She had forgotten everything as his mouth moved caressingly on hers, and her body had strained to fit itself closer to his. Another shiver ran down Fran's spine, and her remembrance of that kiss made her cheeks grow hot with shame. What if Martin used it against her?

She pushed that thought out of her mind. O'Brien might be a hard, relentless interviewer, but she had no reason to believe he wouldn't keep his word. Besides, she had not really told him anything damaging.

With a muffled exclamation, she threw back the covers and went to take her shower. It wasn't what she had *said* that bothered her; it was what she'd *felt*. And that, unless she was very careful, could be extremely dangerous.

By the time she and Harriet reached the classroom, Fran hoped she was in control of herself. She didn't want her dealings with the arrogant Mr. O'Brien to be influenced by what had happened with the wonderful Martin of last night. The truce was over.

As she and Harriet entered the room, the class greeted them. The chairs, she noted with pleasure, had already been shoved into a circle. She settled into one, only half noticing that it faced the door.

Harriet moved toward Mr. Wilson and Fran smiled to herself. Wherever she went, Harriet craved the company of men. Fran smiled again as she thought of the humorous list of non-winners she had compiled for her book. Martin probably did belong in the love-'em-and-leave-'em category, as she had first suspected. But being a non-winner didn't mean that he lacked charm. On the contrary, it was usually because of their charm that so many non-winners were able to make women love them and, subsequently, to cause those same women great pain. That was not going to happen to her, of course, because she knew what was going on. Last night had been pleasant, a fun little adventure. That was all it could be.

She heard the sound of his voice in the hall and her body responded, longing to be in his arms.

"Well, here we are," O'Brien said cheerfully as he entered, followed by Charlie. His eyes went to the clock. "And with minutes to spare."

She couldn't help herself. Her mouth curved into a smile of welcome and her eyes searched his for...she was not sure what. But whatever it was, she couldn't find it. His eyes remained cool.

"Good morning, Miss Warren."

There was a definite lilt to his voice but that could have been caused by anything. "Good morning, Mr. O'Brien." She glanced at the clock. "Will you please get your cameraman in position? I'd like to begin on time."

"Of course, Miss Warren."

Why did she feel he was snickering at her? And what could he be laughing about? But there was no time now for such considerations. The class was waiting.

"Do all of you have your assignments ready?" she asked. There was a chorus of affirmative replies.

"Good. Then let's begin."

With a sense of shock, she noticed that Harriet had moved around the circle and was now seated next to O'Brien. For a moment she almost lost her train of thought. Then, realizing everyone was looking at her, she continued speaking. "I want one of you to start by reading your title and statement of purpose. Then the rest of us will give you our opinions. Do we have a volunteer?"

This time Mrs. Crawford looked as if she wanted to sink through the floor, Mr. Wilson appeared thoughtful, and the teen-aged boys looked apprehensive. It was Mrs. Parker who said, "I'm game."

"Fine." Fran hoped her relief wasn't too obvious. Martin's...no, O'Brien, she corrected herself. O'Brien's being there was putting a big strain on her.

"All right." Mrs. Parker's eyes sparkled. "What do you want first?"

"The title," Fran replied. "Then we can consider it while you read the purpose, to see if they fit each other."

Mrs. Parker nodded. "Okay. I'm having some trouble with the title, so if anyone has any suggestions I'm willing to listen. I'm thinking of something like *Live A Happy Old Age.*" She grimaced. "I hate those words—old age. Don't like senior citizens, either. Anyway, here's the statement of purpose: as modern medical care gives more people longer lives, more of us face mandatory retirement, and/or being widowed. Often we need help to realize that life can still be wonderful. My book will offer step-by-step instructions on what to do if one is widowed, lonely, forced to retire, et cetera. The basic idea behind all the suggestions is that of helping other people. Each chapter will approach it somewhat differently. All the ideas in it have been tested. I've used them all, for myself and for my friends." She looked at Fran and paused.

"Very good, Mrs. Parker. That's the kind of presentation I like. Now, class, let's have your response."

"I don't like the title, either," Mr. Wilson said. "But the book sounds like a great idea." He looked a little sheepish. "Your husband is a lucky man."

"He was," Mrs. Parker said with a tight smile. "I lost him a long time ago." Her smile turned grim.

"That's how I came to develop a lot of ideas. I needed 'em."

Mr. Wilson nodded. "I know what you mean. It's hard being alone."

"It's hard for widowed people whatever their age," Don added. "I saw what my mom went through."

"And younger people can lose those they love, too, whether through divorce or some other way," Harriet added.

Fran turned to her volunteer. "Well, Mrs. Parker, what do these comments suggest to you?"

Mrs. Parker smiled again. "Sounds like maybe I'd have a wider audience if I dropped the age stuff and just talked about being alone and lonely and what to do about it."

Don's friend Tony snapped his fingers. "That's it!" he cried gleefully. "Right there's your title!"

Mrs. Parker looked startled. "Where?"

"You just said it: *Alone and Lonely: What to Do about It.*"

Don beamed and clapped his friend on the shoulder. Mrs. Parker looked speculative.

Fran, who was finally beginning to relax a little, sighed in relief. One of the hardest things in a class composed of people so far apart in age was getting them to relate to each other, and to work together. What had just happened would unite the class and help them all achieve their goals.

She risked a glance in O'Brien's direction and found him looking at her. She wrenched her eyes away, aware that she had hoped to see admiration in his face, but he was expressionless. She swallowed her disappointment and reminded herself that this was O'Brien she was dealing with today, a far cry from the wonderful Martin of last night.

"You know, young man," Mrs. Parker began, then paused. "I mean, Tony, I like that idea. You're one smart fellow. Thank you."

Tony glowed. "Miss Warren," he said, "isn't there some way we can all keep in touch and find out if someone gets his book published? If Mrs. Parker gets this book out, I'd sure like to read it."

Heads were nodding around the circle and Fran smiled again. "I think that can be arranged, Tony. Anyone who wants to..."

"We all do," came a chorus of interruptions.

"You can put your names and addresses on a mailing list," Fran continued. "Mine will be on it, too. And I promise if..."—she stopped—"...no, *when* someone gets a book accepted, I'll let the rest of you know."

"That's great," Don said.

"Yeah," Tony added, "you're a real nice lady."

Fran, accepting this in the spirit in which it was offered, smiled. "Any more comments on Mrs. Parker's book proposal?" The class remained silent. Fran turned to the woman. "If you decide to incorporate this feedback, you'll need to change your statement of purpose and probably your table of contents."

Mrs. Parker nodded her white head. "No sweat," she replied, causing a ripple of amusement around the circle. "My mind's going a mile a minute." She glanced at Tony. "But I'm going to put all that on hold for a while. I want to give my share of help to the rest. In fact, I think I'll use some of this experience in one of my chapters.''

"The one on attending classes, I suppose." It was the first time O'Brien had spoken, and the class turned to him in surprise, most of them having apparently forgotten his presence.

"Maybe," Mrs. Parker replied coolly.

Fran sighed. Mrs. Parker might be willing to accept the two long-haired young men in faded jeans, but she was obviously still suspicious of O'Brien. And with proper justification, Fran thought sadly. What a pleasure this class would have been without O'Brien's intrusive presence. And yet, his very presence could be the catalyst that was bringing the class together. A common threat always made differences seem less significant.

By mid-morning Fran was feeling more relaxed about O'Brien. Aside from his one comment to Mrs. Parker, he had remained silent. Fran glanced at her watch. "Time for a break," she said. "See you in fifteen minutes sharp. I'd like to finish discussing everyone's assignments today."

The students rose from their chairs and headed for the lounge and the free coffee there. Fran stood up and turned her back to the circle. From the corner of her eye she had seen Harriet approach O'Brien and she had no desire to see him in action.

"Miss Warren." His voice was so close to her that she jumped and almost fell backward into his arms.

"Hello, Mr. O'Brien," she said, turning and trying to appear calm.

"I'd like to use this break for a little on-camera chat. Sort of a rehearsal for our interview. Do you mind?"

Of course she minded. But his request seemed legitimate. "I suppose not. As long as we don't use class time."

O'Brien's eyes were unreadable. "Agreed," he said. "Shall we sit down?"

Fran resumed her seat, her nerves tingling. It was weird to deal with this O'Brien, remembering the hours she had spent dancing in Martin's arms.

O'Brien nodded to the cameraman. "Okay, Charlie. Now, Miss Warren, let's talk about your book. It's rather controversial, is it not?"

"I suppose you could say that." Fran chose her words carefully, trying to avoid any traps he might be laying for her. "Although I think controversial is too strong a word. I think provocative is a better choice because the book provokes thought." The words came smoothly and she gave O'Brien a smile, the professional smile of one who continually talks to strangers. "Actually, the book is based on the latest scientific findings concerning human beings and the relationships between them."

She had been over this many times before, but never with a man like O'Brien, and never with the feeling that she would like to forget the whole thing and run off with her tormentor! "People always relate to each other, whether consciously or unconsciously," she continued, the familiar words suddenly sounding strange to her ears. "I simply explain how these things work."

"In fact, do you not explain how women can trap men into marriage?"

"No," she replied firmly, "I do not. There is nothing relevant to entrapment in my book."

"My dear Miss Warren"—O'Brien's eyes gleamed as he closed in for the kill—"may I remind you of the chapter that tells how to get a man to propose?"

She was ready for that one; it was the chapter that had infuriated many male interviewers. "May I remind *you,* Mr. O'Brien, that the chapter does not tell *how* to get a man to propose, but how to discover *if he's ready to.* There is a considerable difference."

"That's right, Mr. O'Brien," Mrs. Parker said smugly. "I read the book."

To her surprise, Fran saw that the class had returned and had been listening with interest to her and O'Brien.

"What it boils down to," O'Brien said, "is a set of chapters outlining a woman's wiles. This scientific view-point is just a cover-up."

"Mr. O'Brien..."

"But," he continued, overriding her attempt to object, "I'm a fair man."

Mrs. Parker snorted and the class burst into laughter.

"I'm a fair man," O'Brien repeated firmly. "And I'm willing to give you a chance to lay your theories on the line."

"I have," Fran replied. "In my book."

O'Brien shook his head. "No," he said. "I mean in real life. I'm offering you a challenge, Miss Warren. You prove your theories work and I'll believe you."

"Prove?" She couldn't comprehend what he was getting at.

"Yes," he continued, his eyes sparkling. "You use your techniques on some man, and see if you can 'catch' him." He smiled and her knees trembled. "And I'll use the natural method to do the same. We'll see who succeeds."

"Wait a minute..." she began.

"You don't have to get him to marry you," O'Brien said with a grim chuckle, "since our time is necessarily limited, of course. But you do have to get him to go out with you and become interested in you. The same applies for me with a woman."

"But these people will know," Fran objected.

"Don't worry, I've got that all figured out." His grin was definitely wicked. "We'll each write the name of the person we choose on a slip of paper, seal it in an envelope, and give it to Mr. Wilson to hold. As a former banker, he seems the best choice."

"It's hardly fair to experiment on people," Fran replied, but her mind was already racing. She could choose O'Brien himself. The man badly needed to be taught a lesson. "And besides, this is your home turf. How do I know you don't already have someone drooling over you?" She hadn't meant to be quite so graphic in her choice of words, but the laughter of the class seemed to back her.

"We'll choose someone who doesn't like us," he said. "Doesn't that seem fair?" He turned to the class for confirmation.

"Well..." She didn't want to seem too eager. "This is not very scientific. An experiment shouldn't be conducted in such an offhanded manner."

"Come on, now, Miss Warren." O'Brien's eyes were mischievous. "No more excuses. Either put up or shut up."

Mrs. Parker gasped and Mr. Wilson glared at O'Brien. But Fran merely smiled. "All right, Mr. O'Brien," she said confidently. "I'll accept your challenge, subject to the objections I have already raised."

"They've been duly noted," O'Brien said dryly.

She was suddenly conscious of the camera pointing at her. "And how will the winner be decided?" she asked.

"I'm willing to leave it up to the class," O'Brien said.

Fran could only stare at him. Surely the man was aware that the class was on her side, that they wanted to protect her from him. "And how long will this experiment last?"

"How about until a week from today?" O'Brien asked. "Can you make someone fall in love with you in a week?"

"Can you?" she shot back, and she was instantly sorry. This was definitely unprofessional conduct. If she hadn't already decided to choose O'Brien himself, she would have refused this challenge, regardless of the consequences. For a moment she suffered a twinge of compassion for the woman O'Brien meant to work on. Even if this woman didn't like him, his fatal charm would not be easy to resist. She knew that from experience.

O'Brien smiled and reached inside his pocket. "I have two empty envelopes and two blank file cards. As you can see, I came prepared."

Fran stared at him. This class was becoming like a circus and it had to stop. "One more stipulation, Mr. O'Brien."

He paused. "Yes?"

"Until the day of reckoning there will be no more discussion of my book in this classroom. You are free to attend meetings, but only as another student."

The look in his eyes made her wary. She realized suddenly that he had anticipated this reaction on her part, but he didn't care. Now that he had what he wanted, he probably wouldn't return to class anyway.

"Of course, Miss Warren," he replied, with a smile so dazzling that her heart turned over. "That seems fair. But I can participate in the class if I hold to your stipulation, can't I?"

She was torn. It would be much easier to practice the techniques in her book on him if he came to class. Yet, in fairness to her students, she should probably not allow him to attend.

Mrs. Parker cleared her throat. "As a student in this class, I have to admit that I resent Mr. O'Brien's intrusion as a reporter. But if he really wants to write a book, I think the story behind his interviewing techniques would be fascinating."

O'Brien's smile grew more charming. "Why, thank you, Mrs. Parker."

"Don't speak too soon, young man," Mrs. Parker warned. "If you're really serious about this thing, you'll pay your tuition and work like the rest of us." The class nodded in approval.

"That's right," Mr. Wilson agreed. "It's only fair."

To Fran's surprise, O'Brien's smile didn't waver. "I think you're right," he replied. "I'll see Mr. Pettigrew right after class." His eyes sought Fran's, and she had to struggle to keep from smiling. Doubtless Petty would find this development the final indignity, and Martin was well aware of it.

Chapter Six

True to his word, Martin O'Brien arrived in class the next morning armed with a receipt and a briefcase. "Good morning," he said cheerfully, handing her the receipt. "Everything's in order."

"How did Mr. Pettigrew take it?" Fran couldn't help asking.

O'Brien chuckled. "The poor old fellow nearly had apoplexy at the thought of having me around for so long. But what could he do when I was standing there with my money in my hand?"

In spite of herself, she smiled. "Mr. Pettigrew leads a life of worry." She was aware of a sudden, insane urge to step into O'Brien's arms and she suppressed it immediately. "And he can hardly be unaware that you're in a position to do the conference some harm."

One of his dark eyebrows shot up. "*Some* harm?" he said. "He knows I could blow the whole thing to pieces."

"Really?" This was going to be more difficult than she had thought. How was she going to get back the Martin she'd danced with? "Such power carries a lot of responsibility," she commented, aware that this was probably not going to help her approach.

To her surprise, he nodded in agreement. "Yes, it does," he replied. "But it also carries a lot of potential for doing good."

"Such as warning people away from things like my book, I suppose!" she snapped, wondering what was driving her to act this way. She was not following her own advice.

He looked rather startled. "More like giving people the chance to see two sides of an issue. Say"—he eyed her speculatively—"I thought your book was off limits here."

"It is," she said hastily. "That was my fault."

He nodded. "Listen, I know I've really been hard on you. Maybe I haven't been fair."

It was her turn to raise an eyebrow.

"I'd like to make it up to you." His brown eyes radiated warmth. "I'd like to show you some of Memphis," he continued, "starting with Mud Island. Are you busy this afternoon?"

"Well..." Be careful, she warned herself. Don't be too eager or he'll know that you've chosen him. "I'm not sure." She grinned mischievously. "Won't you need the time for other things?"

He picked up her cue and shook his head. "No, I've finally settled on my target. But she's not available until tomorrow." His grin was arrogant. "It's hard to find a woman who doesn't like me, you know."

"Yes," she said, trying to keep her voice objective. "I suppose it is. You certainly *look* good."

"Then it's a deal," he said, ignoring the sarcasm in her last remark. "I'll pick you up around one." He lowered his voice. "Just you, you understand. I don't owe anything to your fancy friend and I don't want her along."

The intensity of his voice alerted something deep inside her, but she was so overwhelmed by her feelings of relief that she ignored it. She told herself that she was relieved only because it would be so much easier to put her plan into action without Harriet there; it had nothing to do with jealousy.

"Why don't I meet you at the library, then?" she said softly. "That might be easier."

"Sounds great. See you then." O'Brien turned to take his seat and Fran brought her thoughts back to the classroom. There was time enough later to decide what to wear.

She set out for the library that afternoon wearing a pale green cotton blouse with a matching wraparound skirt and sandals. She had pulled her long blond hair into a ponytail and tied it with a green ribbon.

Since O'Brien clearly didn't like the sophisticated type, she would be careful not to appear as one. Actually, she had always felt that the ultra-fashionable look required too much time and energy. Long ago she had decided that the girl-next-door image was more her style. Now she felt quite comfortable that way.

She reached the library and paused to look around. The campus was old and lovely, and the library had its own quaint charm.

"I see you're prompt," O'Brien said from behind her. "A useful habit."

"One ingrained by years in the academic community," Fran replied, turning to face him. Once again he was wearing slacks and a sport shirt open at the throat. Wisps of dark chest hair curled out of that opening and she wondered with a hint of irritation if he wore his shirt that way on purpose.

"Nevertheless, it certainly makes life easier." His teeth gleamed under his dark mustache as he smiled at her. "My car's over there. Just a short walk and we'll be in air conditioning again."

Fran realized with a little sense of shock that the heat no longer bothered her. "Oh, I guess I'm getting used to it," she replied. "Having sunshine every day is marvelous."

As O'Brien guided her to the car, the feeling of his hand on her elbow sent tremors through her entire body. Be careful, warned her mind. This one is very dangerous.

"Not so much sun where you live?" he inquired conversationally.

"No, not at all. We get a lot of cloudy days in Cleveland due to the lake effect."

"I see. Well, you're dressed right for Memphis. And you look like a teen-ager."

He opened the car door and waited to close it behind her. The red-carpet treatment, she thought. Obviously, the sexual attraction between them had not been one-sided. Martin had felt it, too; she was sure of that.

"I understand Mud Island is a museum," she said, trying to pull her mind away from such thoughts. "Is that right, Mr. O'Brien?"

His right hand left the steering wheel and closed over hers. She felt that same shiver of delight. "Could we call another truce?" he asked softly. "Martin and Fran had a good time the other night. So why don't we leave Mr. O'Brien and Miss Warren in the classroom and be Martin and Fran today?"

He was playing right into her hands, she thought. For a moment she felt guilty. She truly liked Martin and she really didn't want to hurt him. But that obnoxious part of him did need to learn a lesson. Maybe after this, he would be more considerate of people.

She smiled gently and squeezed his fingers. Then, matching her tone to his, she replied softly, "I think that's a great idea. After all, Fran and Martin deserve to have some fun."

"That's right," he said, returning his hand to the steering wheel and backing smoothly out of the lot. "And fun is what we're going to have. But first a little background information. Technically speaking, Mud Island is not just a museum. It also has a scale model of the entire Mississippi River, shops and restaurants, and a playground for kids."

"Mud Island," she remarked. "That's a funny name."

"I guess it's just truthful." He chuckled. "Through the years the city has tried many times to change it to something else. But nobody pays attention. We just go on calling it Mud Island."

He gave her a quick glance and she felt her heart pounding. She not only looked like a teen-ager, she felt like one.

"Along here," he said as they turned a corner, "is Beale Street. The home of W.C. Handy and the blues. The city is doing a lot of renovation here of old theaters, restaurants, and shops. There's Handy's statue over there in that little park. Do you like jazz?"

"Yes, especially the trumpet and the sax." She smiled ruefully. "My education didn't include much about music, but I do know what I like."

"How about that!" he said, raising one of those dark eyebrows. "We actually have something in common."

"I guess miracles do happen," she said mischievously. "At least sometimes."

"I guess so," he agreed, pulling into a parking garage by the river. "Not afraid of heights, are you?"

"No. Why?"

"Because to get to Mud Island we have to ride a cable car. It's fabulous. You can look out over the river or back at the city."

"You love this city, don't you?" she asked as he helped her out of the car.

"I sure do."

"But you weren't born and raised here."

His smile seemed forced. "You mean my southern accent didn't fool you?"

She laughed. "I mean your southern accent doesn't exist. Where did you come from?"

His laughter seemed hollow. "Would you believe New York City?" His tone became lighter. "But enough of that. Memphis is my home now and always will be. I like the sun and I especially like the people."

His glance seemed to include her. "So," he said as he took her hand in his, "Mud Island, here we come."

The view from the cable car was breathtaking. Standing by the windows, Fran looked out over the Mississippi. "What are those tanks on the shore for?" she asked, turning to find Martin so close behind her that she almost jumped.

"Those are oil tanks," he said, slipping his arm around her waist and pulling her back against him. "A lot of tankers travel on the river."

"Oh." She wanted to think of something intelligent to say, but all she could think of was the feel of his arm around her waist and the warmth of his body against her own.

"Beautiful, isn't it?" he said, bending his lips toward her ear.

The afternoon sun had turned the surface of the water to a shimmering sheet of gold. "Yes," she breathed. But it was not the beauty of the river that left her in awe, but the closeness of the man behind her, and the sudden knowledge that without any conscious effort on her part, her heart was beating in time with his. Synchronization technique number five, she thought automatically.

The moment between them passed. With a lot of rattling and clanking the cable car came to a halt. For one second neither of them moved. Then Martin dropped his arm and stepped away. "Do you want to see the museum first, or the shops?" he asked.

"The museum," Fran replied. "I think they're far more interesting than shops, don't you?"

A curious smile crossed O'Brien's face and she wondered what she had done to cause it. But it quickly disappeared as he nodded and took her hand. "The museum it is."

"Oh!" Fran stepped inside the museum and turned to O'Brien. "This is lovely," she declared, looking around at the displays. "All kinds of old things." Again that curious smile crossed his face and then was gone.

They wandered happily in and out of the galleries, gazing at old guns, farm and household implements, and finally pausing before a long wall displaying Currier and Ives prints. "They're all about the Mississippi," Martin said. "Amazingly detailed, aren't they?"

"Oh, yes. Look at this one of people working in the cotton fields along the river. You can actually see the cotton pods."

Martin nodded. "I like this one best."

Fran looked at the print of a paddle wheel steamboat and chuckled. "Martin O'Brien, is it possible that you have a romantic heart?"

He smiled sheepishly. "You won't tell anyone, will you? I don't want to ruin my bad image."

Fran chuckled. "I promise. I'll keep your dark secret all to myself."

He laughed and squeezed her hand. "Fran Warren, you are an absolute gem. Sometimes I even forget that you're a shrink."

From the look in his eyes, she knew that this was more than a casual comment. She kept her tone light as she laughingly replied, "And I had forgotten that you're..."

"Stop," he whispered fiercely. "Remember our truce."

"You broke it this time," she pointed out.

"I did," he said, hanging his head. "I plead guilty. Do I look properly remorseful?"

Fran laughed at him. "You look remorseful? Never!" She felt carefree and light-headed with this man. She couldn't remember the last time a man had made her feel that way.

"Want to go in and watch the movie they have about Currier and Ives?" Martin asked.

What she really wanted to do, Fran realized, was to forget this whole challenge thing and let herself fall madly and passionately in love with this man. But she couldn't do that. Fran and Martin might be having fun today, but in reality they were still Miss Warren and Mr. O'Brien. She had to keep that in mind if she expected to come out of this emotionally in one piece.

She lifted her eyes to his face. "Do you?"

Those brown eyes seemed to be trying to read her mind, and she felt a twinge of regret over what she was doing. She had to be very careful. If he found out what she was doing before the challenge was over, she would lose. She didn't want to be made a fool of in front of her class, and even more important, she didn't want to ruin the pleasure of this day.

Martin shrugged. "I want to please *you*," he said so softly that she couldn't be sure she heard him correctly.

"Let's see the show," she replied, matching his tone.

The little auditorium was softly lighted and a dozen or so people were waiting for the film to begin. "Do you like Currier and Ives work generally?" Martin inquired after they were settled into their seats.

"Yes, I do." Fran chuckled softly. "Though I'm afraid that I'm in the same sad state with art as I am with music. I know very little about the field, but I know what I like. My taste runs more to the realistic. I like pictures that I can understand, especially the ones that tell a story."

Martin nodded.

The lights dimmed and the movie began. By the time it was finished, Fran found herself even more amazed at the two lithographers who had so influenced American taste in art.

As they left the little theater, Martin said, "You're going to love the next section of the museum. It's the ballroom of a steamboat. You can see the bar and there's a little cabin off to one side. Then we can go down the stairs to see the lower deck and a mock-up of the dock."

Hand in hand they wandered through the elegant ballroom, pausing to listen to recorded conversations of the past. Beyond the dock area, life-sized wax figures posed in different tasks. Fran could feel the historical magic of this city. No wonder Martin loved it so.

As they continued through the museum, they saw displays of jazz singers and the honky-tonks where they had played. The replica of a Civil War bunker with its thunder of guns and shouted commands of officers gave her a feeling of great sadness, and she found herself hurrying to get through the rest of the museum.

As they walked outside, Martin smiled down at her. "I hope you enjoyed that as much as I did," he said softly.

"I did. Thank you for taking me. Where do we go now?"

She was very much aware of the pressure of his hand on hers and of the nearness of the body that exerted such a powerful pull on her own. If only she could step into his arms and lay her head on his shoulder, their hearts beating as one. She sighed. Hearts beating as one was the last synchronization technique. It couldn't very well be practiced in such a public place.

"Now we can either get something to eat in one of the restaurants, look at the scale model of the river, or browse in the shops." His grin was magic, she thought, trying hard to stay in control and knowing that it was impossible. He made her feel as if she was sixteen years old and having her first date with the school football hero. Her feet hardly seemed to touch the ground especially when she noticed the envious way other women were looking at them.

"I—I don't want to take up too much of your time..." She faltered, aware that she would like nothing better, but not wanting to seem too eager. Hadn't she advised her readers against the dangers of that very thing?

He smiled with amusement. "I've set aside the entire day for making amends," he replied. His eyes met hers and a shiver traveled down her spine despite the ninety-degree temperature. "You wouldn't want to interfere with my moral development, now, would you?"

She tried to look serious, but couldn't help laughing. "No, no. I wouldn't want to do that."

"Good. Then we'll see everything here." The brown eyes darkened. "Unless, of course, you have other plans."

"No," she replied cautiously. She had never been a good liar, and lying to Martin was almost impossible. "I'm not starting my...campaign until tomorrow, either."

"Great." The heartiness of his reply seemed forced. "You can make a new man of me."

She laughed again. "Isn't that rather a tall order? A new man in one day?"

He grinned. "Maybe. But I have confidence in you."

"Okay." There was something about this line of conversation that bothered her, some underlying sadness in his voice. "Then let's start with the model of the Mississippi."

"Your wish is my command." He tucked her arm through his. "Shall we go upriver or downriver?"

"You make that choice," she said, still smiling.

"Then we'll start at the source and follow it down to the sea."

"Lead on."

How strange this whole thing was, she thought, as she moved beside him. If she had met Martin O'Brien in some other way, she never would have suspected that this charming, gentle man could have such a harsh side to his nature. A regular Dr. Jekyll and Mr. Hyde, she thought, but an extremely fascinating man. There was a mystery about his past, something that kept him from leaving this city that, however charming, was not really his home.

"I hear that you've been offered some wonderful jobs in New York and L.A.," she commented. "Why do you stay here?"

He frowned and the Martin she knew vanished for a moment. Then he managed a smile. "Ever hear of the Peter Principle?" he asked. "I don't want to advance to the level where I'm incompetent."

She shook her head. "But these are the same kind of jobs that you have."

"Then let's just say that I'd rather be a big frog in a small pond than a small frog in a big pond."

She was tempted to push the subject further, but something in his face stopped her. "Sorry," she said. "I think I just bent our agreement."

His smile lightened. "It's okay, Fran." He squeezed her arm. "I won't even ask a leading question in return. See how my character has developed already. You *are* a miracle worker."

She smiled sadly. If she really were a miracle worker, she knew what she would do: she would fix it so that Martin and Fran could be together forever. The thought hit her with such force that she was afraid her face would give her away. She avoided his eyes and stared down at the model.

"All these little levels represent the levels of the Mississippi's bottom," Martin said, and she tried dutifully to look interested.

They traveled the rest of the distance to the river's mouth in silence. "Now," Martin said, as they reached the model's end, "shall we see what the shops have to offer?"

"Yes." Fran tried to sound enthusiastic, but Mud Island seemed to have very little significance for her now. She was becoming more and more obsessed with Martin O'Brien. He was far more fascinating than anything that could be found on a sightseeing trip. And, she admitted to herself with a small sigh, it was not because she wanted to win the contest. In fact, she was sorry now that she had consented to it. There was more to Martin O'Brien than appeared on the surface, and she wanted to learn all about him without worrying about the challenge.

For instance, what was it that anchored Martin O'Brien to this particular city? And why did he dislike sophisticated women?

She sighed. There was no way, of course, that she could get answers to her questions. Not now, at least.

It was clear to her that Martin O'Brien was a very private person. To get at his secrets would be no easy matter; it would take time to gain his trust. And time, unfortunately, was one thing she did not have.

Chapter Seven

Later, sitting across the table from Martin in the waterfront restaurant, Fran felt like pinching herself. The day had been filled with one good thing after another: first Martin's unusually good behavior in class; then their afternoon together; and now dinner.

"I hope you don't mind eating early," he said softly. "I want to be sure we get to the *Memphis Queen* on time."

Fran looked at him curiously. "No, I don't mind an early dinner. And this is a lovely place. But what is the Memphis Queen?"

His eyes sparkled. "No visit to Memphis is complete without a trip on a paddle wheel steamboat. You did say you were free this evening, didn't you?"

"I didn't say exactly that," she protested.

"But you will go with me, won't you? It's a wonderful way to end the day. It really gives you some of the flavor of the old South."

"But Harriet..." she began.

A shadow crossed his face. "Your friend can get along by herself."

"Yes, but I am supposed to be visiting with her."

"Visit when you get back. I won't keep you late, I promise."

She was surprised to see a pleading look on his face. It was not that she didn't want to go with him; she did, very badly. It was only that she felt guilty leaving Harriet alone so much after the arrangements they had made to be together. "I'll call her," Fran compromised, "and tell her I'll be a little later than I'd planned."

Martin's smile could only be called triumphant, and Fran experienced a sense of uneasiness that she ignored. He was playing right into her hands. She did, after all, have her reputation to uphold, and her standing in the classroom. And of course, she had to be with him to use her techniques.

She smothered a sigh. Why did things have to be so complicated? Why couldn't she have met Martin some other way, without being the target of his aggressive TV interviewing? So many things were right between them.

It's only the chemistry, her mind told her sharply. But in her heart she knew that wasn't exactly true. There was definitely more than chemistry between them. There were many things she liked about Martin.

She might not agree with him about his handling of interviews, but she was becoming more convinced that he was a man of principle. When he did something, he did it because he felt it was right. She could certainly respect that. People were, after all, entitled to their convictions. And Martin was certainly standing by his.

"A penny for your thoughts," he teased.

Fran surveyed the seafood salad the waiter had set in front of her. "Sorry," she said. "I'm afraid my thoughts are off limits."

"Oh, dear," he said, shaking his head, "don't tell me you were thinking about that awful O'Brien." He grinned at her and her body tingled. Yes, the chemistry was definitely there.

He reached across the table to squeeze her hand. "Forget about him. Today he doesn't exist. Just think about poor Martin, here, who wants to please a lovely lady."

His smile turned wistful. "Not many people get to see this Martin, you know. Even I hardly do. In fact, I thought he was pretty well dead and buried."

Fran stared at him, unable to think of a single thing to say. It was clearly too important a moment to say the wrong thing, and she was afraid that anything she might say would break the spell.

He laughed and she winced at the bitterness that laughter held.

"Well," he said, "the old Martin still exists. At least he does for you."

He seemed to expect some reply and she finally found her voice. "I'm honored," she said quietly.

For a moment he looked uncomfortable. Then he glanced at his watch and smiled charmingly. "Enough true confessions. We'd better eat if we don't want to miss the boat."

She acknowledged this last remark with a chuckle. "The seafood salad is delicious," she said. "And I like the atmosphere here."

"Yes. I like to watch the river." He grinned, his good spirits evidently revived. "Now we had better eat fast. I'm determined to end our day with a trip on the *Memphis Queen.*"

Obediently, Fran bent her head and gave her attention to her food, but she felt her uneasiness return. This day with Martin had been wonderful, but it didn't make much sense. Clearly, he had not changed his mind about her book. Yet he wanted to spend this day with her, and he was enjoying it as much as she was. Now he wanted to take her for a ride on the steamboat. She wondered what was going on.

As she ate, she remembered the Currier and Ives prints they had looked at. The old South had been so romantic: women in colorful crinolines and gowns, and men in dashing outfits with swords and pistols. For a moment she pictured Martin in a dark costume similar to the one Clark Gable had worn in *Gone with the Wind*. Even his mustache fit, she thought with amusement. He would have made an extremely attractive southern gentleman.

Face it, Fran, she told herself, Martin O'Brien would be attractive no matter what he wore. But she could not forget who Martin really was, or what he could do. If she did, she'd be sorry. That was one fact about which there could be no doubt.

They finished their dinner quickly. "The sunset is gorgeous here," Martin said. "But it's better out on the water."

Fran nodded. She could not understand why Martin O'Brien wanted her to see the sunset. Perhaps he was trying to show her why he loved this city and refused to leave it. But there was another reason, something he had said. She searched her mind for it as they traveled back to the car and then eased into the traffic.

He had said something about loving the place. That she could clearly remember. But there had been more to the sentence, something about...loving a place or someone in it! That was it! There was a *person* who kept Martin O'Brien in Memphis. She would bet on it.

Stop right there, she told herself. You've done more than enough betting as it is. Your job is to get Martin O'Brien interested in you to prove your theories. It's not necessary to pry out the man's secrets.

If only Martin wasn't so intriguing! If he ever did open up, it would be a triumph for the woman in his life. But that woman won't be you, she reminded herself. Leave the poor man with his secrets intact. At least have that much courtesy.

"Here we are," Martin said. "Right on time. And there she is."

The riverbank slanted sharply down to the water, where the white paddle wheel with the red trim glistened in the late afternoon sun. Martin opened the car door. "Better let me help you," he said in a soft, intimate tone. "The gravel here is big and awkward to walk on."

"Thank you, Martin."

His eyes gleamed as she said his name and she could sense the desire reflected in them. The man exerted such power over her. If only he hadn't issued that stupid challenge. Tomorrow, or maybe even later tonight, he would be charming some other woman. A sharp pang of jealousy told her clearly how she felt about that.

She must be losing her mind, she thought, as they walked down the riverbank, his arm holding her tightly. No matter how appealing Martin was now, this was only part of the man. The other part—the harsh, cynical O'Brien—infuriated her. But it was hard to remember that when his arm was around her waist, making her think ridiculous thoughts.

She was so busy thinking that she forgot to pay attention to where she was going. Her sandal slipped on one of the larger stones, throwing her sideways. In a state of panic she grabbed him, but it wasn't necessary. He had already turned to face her, pulling her into his arms and close against his chest.

She could only stand there, trembling violently, her face buried in his shirtfront, her hands clutching at him.

"Are you okay?" he whispered into her hair.

"Yes," she whispered against his chest. She dared not lift her eyes to his, when every nerve ending in her body was alerted to the feel of him. She breathed deeply, trying to calm her nerves, and instead inhaled the heady masculine scent of him. Her bones had

turned to Jell-O and she seemed incapable of moving.
You've got to stop this, she told herself angrily. You're
being absolutely ridiculous. This man is a no-win
proposition, and you know it. So it feels good to be in
his arms. So what?

Her thoughts restored her to a proper perspective.
"Thank you," she murmured, trying to ease herself
out of his arms. "I'm all right now."

He did not let her go. "Are you sure?" he asked.
"You're trembling like a leaf."

"I'm sure. It just startled me." She tried again to
draw back, conscious that his heart was beating in
rhythm with hers again. Or hers with his. Who could
tell for sure? But still he did not release her.

"Look at me," Martin said. "Let me see your
face."

This was the last thing Fran wanted to do when his
face was so near her own. But his voice carried au-
thority and she knew that if she didn't look at him, he
wouldn't release her. She smiled brightly and tried to
still the pounding of her heart. His was beating just as
hard; she could feel it against her cheek.

She lifted her face. "See? I'm fine."

His eyes searched hers, until she felt that her soul lay
exposed to him. The feeling brought on a surge of
panic. He mustn't know how she felt.

"Come on," she said, trying not to think about the
mouth so close to hers. "We don't want to miss the
boat."

His eyes held hers for another long moment before
his arms loosened. "All right. But step carefully. Make
sure your ankle's all right."

"I will." Fran was not sure if she felt disappointment or relief as she moved out of the protective circle of his arms. She probably felt a little of each, she thought wryly as his arm slid around her waist again.

"Take it easy now," he said, and she forced herself to concentrate on walking to the gangplank without any more accidents. She tried not to think about the fact that her ankle was not all right, but was throbbing painfully.

Only when they reached the river did she allow herself to raise her eyes. The *Memphis Queen* was not a large boat, not big enough to hold the saloon, ballroom, and cabins she had seen in the museum. But its fresh white paint and red trim gave it a festive air.

She waited while he bought the tickets at the small building to the right, and then accepted his arm gratefully as they moved to board the paddle wheel.

"Does your ankle hurt?" Martin asked shrewdly.

"A little," Fran admitted. "But there's nothing seriously wrong, I'm sure. I just wrenched it a bit."

He frowned. "Do you think you can make it up to the top deck? We can see more from there. If we want seats, we really should go up right away, before they're all gone."

She followed his gaze back to the riverbank and saw that a number of cars were already parked and that more were arriving.

"It's a very popular thing to do on a summer evening," he explained.

"I can see that." She turned back to him. "Let's go up on top, then. My ankle's getting better all the time. I don't want to miss anything."

"Good. This way."

The narrow staircase ran up the outside of the boat, from the door to the glassed-in portion of the main deck, to the open upper deck, where rows of chairs were arranged. Martin led her toward the edge of the back row. "We should be comfortable here. You'll have a good view of the river."

With his help Fran managed to lower herself into the chair. She was not quite successful in hiding her sigh as she rested her ankle. But fortunately Martin was busy getting himself settled and didn't notice.

Fran tried to distract herself by looking at a large flat barge that was being pushed down the river by a small tugboat. The tugboat looked ridiculous pushing such an enormous load. She smiled, remembering a story she had read as a child about the tugboat that always got the dirty jobs until it proved its worth by rescuing an ocean liner.

Impulsively, she turned to the man beside her. "Martin, do you remember the story about the tugboat?"

"The one that saved the ocean liner?" he replied absently, his eyes still on the river.

"Yes, that's the one." A shared childhood memory, she thought. Very good.

"It's one of Joanie's favorite stories."

She wanted to ask who Joanie was, but the sudden expression of dismay on his face stopped her.

"The tugboat's name is *Tuffy*," he went on. "Joanie is my...sister's girl."

Regretfully, Fran turned her attention back to the river. Whoever Joanie was to Martin O'Brien, she was not his niece. Fran could perceive a lie when she was told one. But why would he lie about a little girl?

"There's a lot of transport on the river," Martin said, changing the subject. "The crews work for three or four months without going ashore."

She knew that he was trying to draw her thoughts away from what he had accidentally revealed, and she found that she wanted very much to help him. She didn't like to see him so uncomfortable.

"Isn't that a long time?" Fran asked, trying to sound curious. "Those boats look awfully small."

Martin seemed more composed now. "I suppose they get used to it."

"How do they eat?" she asked. "I mean, three or four months—that's a lot of food."

"They use the ship-to-shore phone to order, and a grocery boat delivers."

"A grocery boat? I never heard of that." She was glad to see that he seemed fully recovered now. Whatever had bothered him had apparently dissipated.

"There are businesses in Memphis devoted to supplying riverboats. Usually they have warehouses right along the river and their own delivery boats."

Fran smiled. "I never imagined such a life. It sounds like a whole other world."

"I suppose it is." His voice sobered. "There are lots of people leading lives we never dream of." He smiled. "Listen, the captain is starting the engine. We're getting ready to leave. But first, look back that way. See the cable car to Mud Island?"

"Yes, I see it. And the bridge into Arkansas."

They were silent for a few minutes as the boat slowly moved away from the dock. Fran let herself relax and enjoy the new sights and sounds. At least, she relaxed as much as she could with Martin O'Brien sitting there beside her, looking so terribly attractive.

Mr. Pettigrew had been right about that, she thought as she watched the bank recede. Martin was as attractive as the conference director had said he was. How horrified Mr. Pettigrew would be if he found her fraternizing with the enemy like this. Poor Petty. He would never know the joys of a real relationship. He was far too busy worrying to have time to get close to any other person.

Unconsciously, she sighed. She was feeling very close to Martin O'Brien right now. And not only physically.

His fingers closed around hers. "How's the ankle?" he asked.

"Oh, it's fine. Doesn't hurt at all." She realized that it was the truth.

He squeezed her fingers. "That's good. Can I get you anything from inside? A cup of coffee? A candy bar?"

"No, Martin, I'm fine." She was saying his name too much, she knew. But that was intimacy technique number one. And he didn't seem to be bothered by it or even aware of it. Careful, cautioned her mind, you're playing with fire.

There was no denying that, but Fran pushed the thought aside. She was here with Martin and she might as well enjoy it. After all, there was the challenge to consider. She saw now that it was even less important than she had originally thought. The fact that they had to choose someone they disliked destroyed any experimental value. A person did not normally try to make someone fall in love with them unless they had strong feelings for that person. Without those feelings all the techniques in the world would be useless. She wished there were some way she could get Martin to understand that she was trying to further relationships, not trick and deceive people.

Martin slid his arm around the back of her chair. "Nice up here, isn't it?" he observed.

"Yes." She realized that she had not even noticed that the weather had cooled off. The setting sun was still reflecting gloriously on the water, and a soft cool breeze was blowing.

As the riverbank slowly slid past, the captain came on the loudspeaker and began to point out interesting sights along the way. The sound of the paddle wheel, the drone of the captain's voice, and the soothing movement of the boat, all combined to make Fran's eyelids grow heavier and heavier. Twice, they closed and her head jerked. "Sorry," she murmured. "It's almost hypnotic."

Martin smiled. "That's okay. You've had a long day. Why don't you put your head on my shoulder and rest your eyes a little?"

"But then I won't see the river," she protested halfheartedly, her eyes growing heavier.

"It'll only be for a little while," he replied. "I'll wake you when we turn around." He glanced at the sun, which was drawing closer to the horizon. "The sun's almost down now. Dusk isn't the best time to see things. By the time we turn around, the moon will be up and you can see more.''

For a moment Fran felt guilty. She was supposed to be spending her free time with Harriet, not flitting around with Martin O'Brien the whole night. Still, Harriet had seemed to understand. For Harriet a date with a man always took precedence over anything else.

It was her own standards that Fran was ignoring. Usually, if she had arrangements with a woman friend, and a man wanted to see her at the same time, she did not change her plans. The fact that she was now behaving in a way contrary to her own beliefs should have made her more upset than it did.

Well, she told herself as she settled comfortably into the curve of Martin's shoulder, she would consider all this later, when she felt more rested. She let her weary eyes close with a sigh of relief.

"Fran." Martin's voice was low against her ear. "Fran, we're turning around. I want you to see the lights.''

Obediently, she opened her eyes. In her sleep, she had settled into his arms until she was half across his lap. But regardless of the discomfort of such a position, she felt rested.

"I'm awake, Martin," she said, raising her head and pulling herself upright. Away from the warmth of his body she felt the coolness of the night air and she shivered. His arm went around her immediately. "It gets cooler when the sun goes down, especially on the water. Look over there. The moon's coming up.''

His arm pulled her close again and she snuggled gratefully against the heat of his body. The moon was just beginning to climb into the darkened sky.

"Did I sleep long?" she asked.

"Not long," he assured her, his arm tightening around her. He grinned. "I was imagining you in one of those old-fashioned gowns we saw at the exhibit. Rustling crinolines and a wide-brimmed straw hat." He pulled at her ponytail. "With your hair down, of course."

"Of course. And what were you wearing?"

"Me?"

"Yes, you. I imagine you were in this fantasy, too."

He looked suddenly sheepish and she laughed. "I bet you had on a dark suit, like Clark Gable wore in *Gone with the Wind*."

He looked startled. "How did you know that?"

She smiled. "I had a similar fantasy earlier. I think most of America must have formed their ideas of the old South based on that movie." She chuckled. "I myself have seen it at least five times."

"And is your favorite scene when Gable carries Vivien Leigh up the stairs?" he asked quietly.

She swallowed hastily, struggling with the rush of desire that his words evoked. "I–I don't have a favorite scene," she stammered.

"That's okay," he said softly, dropping the subject. "Come stand at the rail with me, will you?"

"Sure." She was pleased to see that her ankle had completely recovered. But she shivered as she approached the railing and the strong breeze brushed against her bare arms.

"Here," he said, wrapping his arms around her so that she stood with her back against his chest, his arms folded over hers. "Umm," he murmured. "Your hair smells good. But that confounded ribbon tickles my nose."

She laughed and withdrew her arms. "Let me loosen it. My hair will help to keep my neck warm."

He blew on her neck, sending shivers down her body. "I'd be glad to do that," he said softly.

She ignored his words and pulled off the ribbon and the elastic tie, letting her hair settle around her shoulders.

"That's better," he said, his arms going around her again. "Much better."

They stood that way for some time, gazing out over the water at the lights twinkling on the opposite bank. And the longer they stood, the more conscious of his body she became. She was sure she could feel his heart pounding against her back and her own thudded in harmony with it. His breath was warm on her ear and the arms that encircled her were wrapped dangerously close to her breasts. She wanted him, she acknowledged, while the blood pounded through her. But there was no way she could act on that desire now. She was not going to sleep with the man and then have him find out that she had chosen him for the subject of their experiment. She simply couldn't do that to Martin.

"Fran." He spoke so softly she almost wasn't sure she had heard him. "Fran."

"Yes, Martin?"

She was never sure whether she turned to face him or whether he turned her. She only knew that suddenly their faces were mere inches apart.

Her heart pounded so loudly in her chest that she was sure he could hear it. His eyes gleamed in the moonlight, and his mouth was close to hers. "I thought about this, too," he said softly, "while you were sleeping."

In fascination she watched his lips approaching hers. Turn your head! Push him away! her mind cried. But Fran simply stood there, awaiting the inevitable. She had known, somewhere deep inside her, that the day would lead to this. Now she rejoiced, raising herself on tiptoes to meet his kiss. His lips were warm and soft as his mouth moved slowly over hers. His arms held her close against his body; she could feel her breasts crushed against his chest, his hard thighs pressed against hers. Her body yearned to be even closer to him and she entwined her arms around his neck and gave herself up to the waves of emotion that flooded over her.

Chapter Eight

The next evening as she waited for the car to take her to the studio for the interview, Fran recalled that kiss and the others that had followed. It was ridiculous of her to feel so good about the whole thing, she told herself. Last night had been a little adventure, a fantasy, a fairy tale. It had nothing to do with the class she had met that morning or the interview Martin—no, she reminded herself—O'Brien would soon be conducting.

It was probable she would never see that Martin again. She frowned. He would no doubt be off, working on the poor, unsuspecting woman he had chosen as his target. Oh, that stupid challenge. If only there were some way she could stop it. But O'Brien would treat any suggestion like that as a concession of defeat. It didn't take a genius to figure that out.

She sighed. The Martin she'd been with yesterday was a wonderful, caring man. The fact that he was also the obnoxious O'Brien seemed almost impossible. But it was quite true and she could be sure that no tender feelings, no amount of kissing in the moonlight, would change that.

She felt the blood racing to her face. There had been kissing in the moonlight, all right, and lots of it. Kissing that had left her so weak she wondered if she'd be able to walk back to the car, or refuse the invitation she felt sure was coming.

But, surprisingly, that invitation had not come. In spite of the passion of their shipboard kisses, Martin had simply returned her to the door of her room, given her a brotherly kiss on the forehead, and said, "I'll see you tomorrow," leaving her standing there with all her unnecessary excuses tumbling through her mind.

She had gone into the room to find Harriet waiting for her. Fortunately, Harriet had not been upset. It was not like her to get upset about anyone's date with a man. The problem had been that Harriet wanted to know all the little details. And she was clearly not satisfied with Fran's description of Mud Island or her observations of the museum and the river.

"Forget that," she had ordered, dismissing such trivialities with an impatient wave of her hand. "Tell me the important part," she demanded. "Tell me how he looked at you, what he said to you, how he touched you."

"Harriet! You're making something out of nothing. Mr. O'Brien is just a nice man who wanted to…"

The expression of amazement on Harriet's face was the first clue to what she had said. "Well, he *can* be nice. He just wanted to make amends for the way he treated me in class."

"Why?" Harriet asked. "I thought that was his usual style. He's certainly good at it."

Fran shrugged. "I don't know why, Harriet. But he really can be very nice. It was a lovely day."

"Aha!" Harriet pounced on her friend's expression. "'Fess up, Fran. He kissed you."

Fran hesitated a moment too long. "Really, Harriet, you ask very personal questions."

"I'm not asking *that* question," Harriet replied, giggling. "I don't have to. It's as plain as the nose on your face. You never could lie to me, Fran. Was he good?"

"Harriet!"

Her friend shrugged. "Well, there's not much sense in getting kissed if the man isn't good. You should know that."

"Really, Harriet..."

Harriet's grin was wicked as she plopped down cross-legged on the other bed. "Come on, sweetie. Tell me all."

"There's not that much to tell. Honestly." Fran acknowledged a sense of disappointment, but only to herself. She had wanted him to invite her back to his place, though she knew she would have had to turn him down. "We visited the places I mentioned. He kissed me and he brought me back here."

Harriet's expression was one of disbelief. "You're kidding!" She scrutinized Fran's face. "You're not kidding. The Memphis lady-killer didn't issue you an invitation. I can't believe it.''

"Neither can I," Fran replied. Then, realizing what she'd already revealed, she pleaded with her friend. "Listen, Harriet, I don't want the class to know about this."

"Oh, Fran, don't feel so badly. It's true he usually hits on blondes, but..."

"Harriet! I don't mean that." Fran's giggle was a little hysterical. "I mean I don't want them to know we went out together. I mean..." She wasn't handling this well and she knew it. "I mean, even if it isn't a regular class, with grades and all, this sort of thing isn't good for morale."

Harriet nodded sympathetically. "I understand." She shook her head. "But I never would have believed that the great O'Brien is not as fast as rumor indicates."

"Rumor can never be trusted," Fran said solemnly in her schoolmarm voice and they both dissolved into laughter.

"I'm sorry to have been gone so long," Fran apologized.

Harriet's smile was genuine. "It doesn't matter a bit. I figured O'Brien would hang on to you after I saw the way he danced with you at the reception. That man's got it bad." She giggled again. "My goodness, Fran! Do you suppose his intentions could be honorable?"

Fran forced herself to join in her friend's laughter. The idea of Martin O'Brien having honorable intentions hit her with such force that she knew there was no sense in denying that she wished it was true. Marriage with Martin O'Brien was exactly what she wanted, no matter how ridiculous the thought was.

"So what did you do this evening?" Fran asked her friend.

Harriet's face turned mysterious. "After you called, I got hold of an old friend and arranged to have dinner."

A certain smugness in Harriet's expression gave away her secret.

"With a man," Fran said confidently.

Harriet stared. "Now, how did you know that?"

Fran grinned. "There's a certain expression you get when you talk about men." Fran giggled. "Like the cat that swallowed the canary. Well, give me all the details."

Harriet looked flustered. "Well..."

Light dawned. "You went to dinner with Ashley."

Harriet nodded. "I didn't think you'd mind. I mean, you said he doesn't mean anything to you."

"He doesn't," Fran assured her. "Not a thing. But I'm afraid I can't be very objective about the man."

Harriet wrinkled her small nose. "My only problem was that I couldn't get him to talk about anything but you. You'd think he'd spent the entire last seven years of his life pining over you."

Fran shook her head. "I wonder if he really left his wife," she mused, "or if *she* left *him*."

Harriet's expression grew thoughtful. "He told me some pretty exhaustive sob stories." She grinned. "And I mean exhaustive. Until I started reciprocating. Every time he mentioned his wife, I mentioned one of my husbands. Eventually, he got the hint and stopped. After that, we had a pretty good time." She glanced down at her ringless left hand. "He's really rather nice."

Fran swallowed and counted to ten. Where Ashley was concerned she was unable to think objectively. "Just be careful," she said finally. "I don't want you to get hurt again."

Yes, Fran thought as she paced around the small room, be careful. Excellent advice; she would do well to heed it herself. She took a deep breath and tried to steady her nerves. This was just a simple TV interview. Even if she bungled the whole thing, or even if O'Brien managed to make her look bad, she would live through it. There was nothing to be so nervous about.

Finally, she faced the truth. It was not her TV appearance that had her stomach tied in knots and her thoughts racing in a thousand directions; it was facing Martin again. He had not appeared in class that day, and the morning had seemed curiously flat. And now she would have to face the indomitable O'Brien before live cameras with the image of Martin lingering in her mind. She straightened her shoulders; she would just have to be prepared for anything.

A tap on the door almost made her leap into the air. It must be the driver. She picked up her purse and opened the door.

"I'm..." The words froze on her lips and she stood there in shock, her purse dropping to the floor.

Martin O'Brien, in an off-white summer suit, stood looking down at her in amusement. "Ready?" he asked.

"Yes. But I didn't...that is..."

"You didn't expect me," he said cheerfully.

She couldn't seem to regain her composure. "You said a driver would pick me up," she finally managed to say.

"Yes, I did. I didn't say it wouldn't be me, though, did I?"

"No, no. You didn't." She picked up her purse with trembling hands and put it quickly over her shoulder, grabbing at the strap to steady her fingers. "I'm ready."

This was all wrong, she thought as they moved down the hall. She didn't want to think of him as Martin when she would soon be face to face with the hot-tempered O'Brien. She needed to put up defenses, not let them down.

"I thought you would be at the studio preparing for the show," Fran said, desperate to attain a business-like tone. "So naturally I assumed you'd send someone for me."

"You should never assume anything," Martin O'Brien said, as he held the heavy door for her. "That's a very dangerous business."

She managed a little laugh. It sounded hollow to her ears, but perhaps he wouldn't notice. The trouble, she thought with sudden clarity, was that she didn't know whom she was dealing with here. Was it the gentle, caring Martin who now took her arm and led her down the sidewalk? Or was it the terrible O'Brien leading the unsuspecting lamb to the slaughter?

Well, she wasn't entirely unsuspecting. And she certainly didn't intend to get slaughtered. The best thing to do was to believe that this was Mr. O'Brien she was dealing with.

"How does your show open, Mr. O'Brien?" Fran asked as they settled into his car.

"With a shot of me, of course," he replied, flashing her a devilish smile. "After all, it is *my* show." He flexed his broad shoulders. "Memphis wants her Golden Boy to live up to his reputation."

She thought she detected a small tinge of bitterness in his voice. But her nerves were so on edge that she couldn't be sure of her perceptions.

He looked at her again. "So it's back to Mr. O'Brien," he said wryly.

"This is business," Fran replied, wondering why she suddenly felt that she had hurt him in some way, "Didn't we agree that Martin and Fran were to be separate from business?"

He frowned. "Yes, we did. But..."

"Please, Mr. O'Brien. No buts. You gave me your word, and I can't believe you'd go back on it."

His eyes seemed almost anxious as he looked at her. "Of course I keep my word." His hand left the steering wheel and moved toward hers, then suddenly returned to the wheel. "It's a good thing for you that I do," he said from between clenched teeth. "Because I'm really tempted to chuck the whole show and just drive off with you. I'd like to take you to some very private place," he said softly, intimately. "Oh, Fran..."

"Please, Martin. Don't. I..." She looked into his eyes and almost lost herself there. "Don't do this to me. I can't handle it."

"You!" His voice bespoke outrage and his knuckles whitened as he gripped the wheel. "What about me?"

"What about you?" she asked softly, already forgetting her resolve.

"I'm supposed to get on camera and rip you apart." He grimaced. "I built my reputation on my razor-sharp wit."

She shrugged. "From what I've seen, it's a reputation well earned."

He frowned. "Of course it is." His eyes held hers.

"So?" She felt that she was holding her breath. The tension between them was terrible.

"So I don't *want* to rip you apart." His frown deepened and his dark eyes grew troubled. "Get this straight. I still don't like the book. I think the whole idea stinks. But..." He hesitated. "But you're different. I think you're a lot like me. Your public persona is very different from the private you. It's the private you that Martin likes," he added so softly that she was sure she hadn't heard him correctly.

"Martin," she said, "it's not the end of the world." Some detached part of her mind looked on with amusement as she consoled the terrible Mr. O'Brien. "You do your job and I'll do mine. What could be more simple?"

"Sure," he said bitterly. "And then you'll hate my guts."

Her laughter pealed out and he turned startled eyes to hers. "Don't be so melodramatic," she chided. "I've been through this before. In fact, I may surprise you. I can make some pretty sharp remarks myself."

"No doubt you can," he said. "But that doesn't solve my problem. Here I am about to publicly rip apart a woman I want to ask to go dancing with me on Beale Street tomorrow night."

"Me?" Her voice faltered as she realized the sudden joy she felt. "You want to take me dancing?"

"Yes, you." He looked slightly uncomfortable. "That is, if you can spare the time from your conquest."

"What about you?" Fran asked softly.

Martin shrugged. "No problem there. I'm doing fine."

She felt a wave of jealousy and tried to ignore it. "Me, too." That, at least, seemed to be the truth. "Listen, I think I have the solution to our problem."

"You do?" He pulled into the station parking lot, turned off the car, and faced her. "What is it?"

"It's simple, Martin." She had not meant to use his first name again since she was not consciously trying to use her techniques on him now. She swallowed hastily. "We'll just agree that nothing that goes on during the course of this interview will affect Martin and Fran."

He looked dubious. "Can we do that?"

"I can," she said softly, touching his hand. "And if I can, you should be able to. After all, I'm the intended victim."

He managed a smile. "But I feel like I am, instead." He sighed. "They're going to run the tape of the challenge, you know. We'll have to talk about that."

She nodded. "I know. We'll still manage."

"Okay," he said, his brown eyes warm. "It's a deal. And we'll go dancing tomorrow night, regardless of anything that goes on during the interview."

"Agreed," she said solemnly.

He nodded, his expression as solemn as hers. "We'll just seal that with a kiss."

Before she could stop him, he had bent and brushed her lips with his. It was only with the greatest effort that she kept from throwing herself directly into his arms.

"I think" he said, his voice husky, "that we'd better go in now, while we still can."

"Yes," Fran said softly. "That's a very good idea."

By the time they reached the studio, she had herself under control. Taking her place in the chair he indicated, she even managed a little smile. "Cheer up," she whispered. "This will soon be over."

"Thank God," he muttered darkly.

Fran smiled and ran through her list of mental preparations as she settled down. She would meet whatever questions O'Brien chose to throw at her. And tomorrow night...

Forget that, her mind warned. Concentrate on this.

The show began and Fran took a deep breath. But when O'Brien began to question her, Fran was startled to find that he didn't seem to be himself. From behind the camera came several seconds of frenzied hand-waving, and still he asked no leading questions.

Finally, Fran took matters into her own hands. "Martin O'Brien disapproves of my book," she said, giving him a cheerful smile. "Will you tell me why, Mr. O'Brien?"

For a long moment she wondered if he would answer at all. Then he seemed to pull himself together. "I disapprove of using techniques on people," he said, "especially in matters of personal relationships."

"Techniques, Mr. O'Brien?" She deliberately goaded him. "I believe the word you used to me was tricks. Sly tricks, if I'm not mistaken."

His eyes looked dangerous as he returned her smile, but she thought she saw him flash her a grateful look. "That's right, Miss Warren. I did. Sly tricks designed to take some poor sucker by surprise."

"And lead him to the altar unaware?" she suggested sarcastically.

"Exactly," he said, matching her tone. "And when the poor guy wakes up, he's already married."

"Your attitude certainly doesn't give the male species much credit for being smart," she replied.

"Intelligence has nothing to do with it," O'Brien protested. "Men are seldom smart where love is concerned."

Something flashed in his eyes only for her to see. Her breath caught in her throat.

"Neither are women, Mr. O'Brien. That's one of the reasons there are so many divorces."

"And you're going to change that?" he asked, his tone disbelieving.

"Now, Mr. O'Brien, don't put words in my mouth," she said, realizing with surprise that she was enjoying this interview. "My book might help women choose a husband, and that might mean fewer divorces. But I don't want to make any claims I can't substantiate."

As she had hoped, he picked up on that right away. "You don't say! But what about the title of your book?" He grimaced. He was in full form now, she thought gleefully. "*How to Catch a Husband: The Scientific Way to Love and Marriage*. Now I ask you, Miss Warren, isn't that a claim? Doesn't the buyer of your book expect to, in your own words, catch a husband?"

He had attacked her and she felt like laughing. This was the O'Brien Memphis expected to see.

"That is not an unsubstantiated claim," Fran replied crisply. "I have files full of letters from women who have used my techniques and found husbands."

"You mean your tricks."

"No, Mr. O'Brien. The techniques described are not tricks. My book is based on proven discoveries about people and the development of relationships."

He shrugged. "What's the matter with nature's way? There seem to have been plenty of marriages before your book came out."

"Of course there were, Mr. O'Brien. And plenty of divorces, too." She realized suddenly that he was feeding her leading questions, giving her a chance to defend her views the way she had done with him. "My hope is that with these new techniques a woman can find the right man and build a good life."

"What, no happily-ever-after?" he asked, his voice sharp.

"There is no happily-ever-after," Fran said softly. "There never will be. Marriage is a partnership, and to make a partnership work there has to be effort from both parties."

To her surprise, Martin nodded. "I'm afraid I'll have to agree with that," he said. "But it's the only thing you've said that I can agree with. This baloney about scientific study and the techniques you describe... I just can't buy it. First of all, scientific study is just that: study. It's not the absolute truth. Scientists are constantly proving their predecessors wrong. The world's flat, then it's round. And the poor guy in the street has to take their word for it!"

He glared at her. "Now you claim that science can tell us how to get someone to fall in love with us. What happened to the old way? To chemistry? To romance?"

His voice softened on the last word and she almost forgot herself and responded to Martin instead of to O'Brien.

"Chemistry and romance aren't gone, Mr. O'Brien. Not at all. There has to be some chemistry or the man won't keep coming back. And as for romance...many people these days are so rushed and so harried by the complexities of modern life that they don't have time for roses and moonlight."

The last word was a mistake; she saw the memory of their evening rise before his eyes and she hurried on. "These are techniques," she repeated, "not tricks."

She tried to smile but found it difficult. What she had to say might make him think of what had happened to them. If he guessed she had used her techniques on him... She pushed the thought away and continued. "If modern science has proven that people in love tend to sit in the same position, walk in step, speak in the same tone of voice, breathe in a symbiotic rhythm, and eventually synchronize their heartbeats, why shouldn't a woman use these things to show a man that she cares for him?"

"Because maybe she doesn't care. Maybe she's faking the whole thing."

For one wild moment she thought she'd been found out.

Then he continued. "Because a cold, uncaring woman could use these same techniques."

He used her word, but his sneering tone made it sound obscene. "She could trap a man into marriage to get what she wants from him. And then when she's wrung him dry, she can just dump him and move on to someone else."

For a moment Fran was left speechless. So this was what had happened to Martin. She knew it as surely as she knew her own name. No wonder he was so bitter.

"Mr. O'Brien, I'm sorry if some unscrupulous women decide to use my book in this way. But I'd like to point out to you that such women were around long before my book was written. And they did very well without it.''

She searched his face, but read only anger there. ''My book is a scientific tool,'' she explained patiently. ''Like any tool, it is neither good nor bad. It can be used to build something or to destroy it. It's the people using the tool who make the good or bad decisions.''

And you've made a bad one, said her mind. Just think how he's going to feel when he finds out that you've used him. She pulled her thoughts back to the present. There would be time to worry about that later.

She paused, waiting for his response. ''An interesting philosophical observation,'' O'Brien said. ''I'll have to give that some thought. But for now, let's take a look at a tape filmed earlier this week in Miss Warren's class at Dow College.''

Aware that the cameras might return to her at any moment, Fran did not look directly at Martin but focused her attention on the studio monitor. There was O'Brien in all his glory harassing her in front of her class. But she was holding her own.

And then he issued the challenge. She wanted to jump up and run from the studio, but she forced herself to sit still and act indifferent. Whatever had possessed her to pick Martin O'Brien as a guinea pig? He would be so hurt when he found out that she'd deceived him that he would never want to see her again. She wondered despairingly how she could possibly live without him.

Chapter Nine

As Fran walked to class the next morning she couldn't stop thinking about the day when Martin would have to find out. He had been so good to her. He had even tempered his questions last night until she had almost forced him into their discussion. And tonight they were going dancing. Her heart leaped.

"Hey!" Harriet's eyes were sparkling. "Do you think the great O'Brien will show up in class today?"

Fran shrugged. "I don't know, Harriet. He didn't say."

Harriet chuckled. "You're really out of it this morning, Fran! You haven't even noticed my hair."

"Sorry. What did Larry do?"

"Larry didn't do anything." Harriet giggled. She twirled around, and her dark hair, loosely waved, swirled out from her shoulders. "I did this myself and it feels great."

"It looks great, too," Fran assured her. "I'm sorry I didn't notice."

Harriet smiled. "Don't worry about it. You've got a lot on your mind. This O'Brien is quite a man."

"Harriet," Fran began, and stopped. She couldn't lie to her friend. "Harriet, I just don't know. I'm really confused."

Harriet sighed knowingly. "Join the club," she said. "I saw Ashley again last night." She paused. "He stopped talking about you after half an hour. Then we talked about me."

"Do you like him?" Fran asked, trying to keep her tone light. She didn't think Ashley was right for Harriet, but Harriet would have to discover that for herself.

"Yes, I like him," Harriet replied. "Sometimes, I mean. I know what he did to you was terrible. And I see things about him that I don't like. But other times..." She sighed deeply. "It's almost like he's two people. One of them I like a lot." She shrugged. "The other I don't like at all."

"Me, too." Fran said with a sigh. "It's like that with Martin. I don't like his TV persona, though I have to admit that the reasoning behind it is legitimate. But the other Martin is so wonderful."

"Oh, oh!" Harriet cried. "I haven't seen that look on your face for a long time. Fran, you've got it bad."

By this time they had reached the building and Fran pulled open the door. "Please, Harriet, just forget what I said. I've got to concentrate on class right now."

"Sure, Fran. I won't say a word." Harriet's usually smiling face was solemn. "Just remember, though, I'm here if you need a friend."

"Thanks, Harriet. That means a lot."

Fran knew that Martin O'Brien was not in the classroom the minute she stepped through the door. She didn't know whether to be relieved or disappointed. Yesterday, when he hadn't been in class, the whole morning had seemed so flat.

She had been disappointed last night when one of the show's crew members had taken her back to the dorm, explaining that Martin would be continuing the show. She had needed to talk to Martin again, to erase the image of O'Brien in full battle array. But the more she thought about it, the more she realized Martin had been very fair. His methods might be harsh, but they were also honest. You knew he was going to attack you and you knew how. She respected him for that.

She sighed as she and Harriet moved the chairs into a circle. She wanted to see Martin, that was all. He hadn't mentioned a time to pick her up this evening, but that really wasn't the issue. She just wanted to see his face, to look into those deep brown eyes.

She brought herself up sharply. Harriet was right: O'Brien was getting to her. She was going to have to be more careful. O'Brien was at least thirty and unmarried. At the moment, anyway. A man that attractive could be single only by choice. Besides, it didn't take much to figure out that matrimony didn't rate very high on his list.

Who was the woman who had taken Martin for everything he had? Fran wondered. She was probably a blonde since the pattern was fairly clear. Martin's wholesale revenge on blondes, his love-'em-and-leave-'em tactics, were due to the hurt his wife had inflicted on him. And his hatred for the techniques in Fran's book suggested that he believed that his wife had never loved him.

Fran sighed again. O'Brien's harsh, cynical attitude could very well be a direct outcome of his failed marriage. She wondered if Harriet knew anything about that marriage, but she decided against asking her. Harriet would put far too much emphasis on such a loaded question.

Fran forced herself to face the facts. All these speculations about Martin O'Brien's character and motives only worked more firmly to put him in the no-win category. It would be foolish of her to let herself love him.

Warmth flooded her whole body and Fran finally admitted the truth to herself. She already loved Martin O'Brien. It was too late to talk about trying not to love him, or to escape with her heart intact.

But maybe they had a chance, she argued silently with herself. Maybe he loved her, too. Together they could work through the problems his wife had caused.

"Good morning, everyone."

Her heart rose up in her throat and threatened to choke her. He was here.

She took a deep breath and forced herself to turn, to meet his eyes. "Good morning, Mr. O'Brien." She worked hard to keep her voice from softening. He must never know what she was thinking.

He crossed the room toward her, followed by the silent Charlie and his ever-present camera. "You're looking very nice this morning, Miss Warren," O'Brien said, his eyes shining. "I must say, battle becomes you."

For some insane reason a giggle rose to her lips. She swallowed it hastily and tried to keep her voice crisp and businesslike as she replied, "Fighting for what's right is supposed to be good for one."

His lips curved into a smile and she found herself wanting to rush into his arms. Instead, she gripped the back of a chair and waited.

"If that's true," he said, "you really must have been right, because you look terrific this morning."

Aware that the classroom was filling up and that her students were staring at them, Fran managed a little laugh. "May I remind you, Mr. O'Brien, that there are no grades given in this class? Buttering up the teacher won't do you any good."

His eyes glistened and for a minute she thought he was going to say something indiscreet, but he only murmured, "Yes, teacher," and turned toward Harriet.

For the first time that morning, Fran really looked at her friend. Not only had Harriet changed her hairstyle to something free and easy, but she had also altered her wardrobe. Instead of the sophisticated dresses and high heels she'd been wearing, she had on faded blue jeans, a simple cotton shirt, and dirty sneakers. The effect, Fran acknowledged to herself, was inviting. While the sophisticated Harriet might have been regarded as aloof by those who didn't know her, this woman radiated warmth. Harriet looked absolutely fabulous, thought Fran with a stab of jealousy.

Martin O'Brien seemed to think so, too. "Good morning, Mrs. Singleton. You're looking very well today."

Harriet glowed. "Thank you, Mr. O'Brien," she said, her voice casual. Just the right tone, Fran thought. "Do call me Harriet. I'm not a Mrs. now, anyway."

"Right, Harriet. So you live in Memphis."

Fran turned away, half angry and half amused by her own reactions. If Martin wanted to make her jealous by paying attention to Harriet, he was succeeding. But she certainly didn't intend to let him know.

On the other hand, she reminded herself, Harriet's new image was very inviting, much more like her real self. O'Brien might well be attracted to her. She tore her mind away from these things and turned to the class. She was not in the classroom to learn about herself, but to teach others.

After the session was over, O'Brien left with nothing more than a cheerful "See you." Fran barely stopped herself from staring after him openmouthed until she remembered that this was her class and she had a reputation to uphold. But she suddenly seemed very tired, and she gathered up her books and notes with a heavy heart. Did this mean that their dancing was off? Surely he would have mentioned what time he was going to pick her up, if, in fact, they were going.

"My goodness," Harriet said impatiently from the doorway. "What is the matter with you? Let's go. I've got things to do this afternoon."

"Coming." Fran pulled the door shut behind her. "Why are you in such a rush?" she asked. "Got a heavy date with Ashley?"

Harriet shook her head. "Not till this evening. But I've got plans for this afternoon. Big plans."

"Oh, going to tell me about them?"

"Fran Warren, you are the most irritating woman. I think being in love has dulled your wits. Now, don't go denying it; I've been there often enough to know. You and I are going shopping this afternoon."

"I don't need anything," Fran quipped.

"Don't need anything?" Harriet stopped and put her free hand on her hip. "Fran, you are completely crazy. Here you are, going dancing with Memphis's Golden Boy, the most eligible bachelor in Shelby County, and you don't need anything?"

"I…" Fran stared. "How did you know about the dancing?"

Harriet grinned. "Why, Martin told me, of course. He said he'd be by to pick you up at seven-thirty. Now, let's hightail it back to the room. We've got a couple of dresses to buy. Old Ashley's taking me out to dinner and I want something simple, but sexy."

Fran laughed. She suddenly felt as if she was walking on air. He'd given his word, hadn't he, that the interview wouldn't change their plans? Why had she doubted him?

She grinned at Harriet. "What are we standing here for? Lead me to the stores."

That evening, as she put on her long, dangling heart-shaped earrings, Fran felt her own heart thudding in anticipation. She was on top of the world: light-headed and giddy. She felt like a girl getting ready for her first prom. Even the dress, which she had finally chosen at Harriet's insistence, was promlike.

She smoothed the soft silky skirt and adjusted the loose neck, which allowed the dress to slip down over one shoulder. By Harriet's old standards it was a very simple dress. It didn't have a wide expanse of bare back or petal-shaped layers of skirts. By Fran's standards, however, it was a little excessive. The new strapless bra she had bought to go with it was surprisingly comfortable, but she still felt strange with her shoulder hanging out.

"The idea," Harriet had said with the mischievous smile Fran remembered so well, "is to look sexy and innocent." So they had spent the afternoon in search of two perfect dresses.

Fran's light lavender one was complemented by low-heeled white pumps. Her flat sandals were not good for dancing, and, besides, the dress, understated as it was, seemed to need more than sandals.

Harriet's dress was simple, too, in everything but its color. It was a smoldering, burnt orange that looked terrific with her dark hair.

Harriet came out of the bathroom as Fran turned once more to pace the length of the little room. "Fran

Warren," she cried, "you're going to wear out the rug like that! Sit down and relax."

"I wish I could."

Harriet chuckled. "I think you'd better reread your book. But maybe not. You seem to be managing real well, anyway."

"Managing?" Fran's mind was elsewhere and she hardly heard her friend's words.

"Fran, honey, you forget. I'm here with you all the time. The only man you've been anywhere near is the fabulous Mr. O'Brien. Therefore, it has to be his name on the paper that dear Mr. Wilson is holding."

"Harriet, stop! I never said..."

Harriet grinned wisely. "There's no need to say. I have eyes. But don't worry, honey. Your secret's safe with me."

A rap on the door made them both jump. Fran sent her friend a warning look and Harriet whispered, "Don't worry. I won't tell."

Several deep breaths on the way to the door helped Fran to regain her composure. When she faced O'Brien, her hand was steady and her smile was almost normal.

"Hello," Martin said, his voice low. Then he whistled softly. "What a dress, and just your color. You look great."

"Thank you." She opened the door. "Step in while I get my wrap."

He was looking absolutely terrific, she thought as she moved back to let him pass her. His pale beige suit set off the bronze of his skin and those sensual brown eyes.

Careful, warned a voice in her head. Get a hold on yourself. You're already in too deep.

"Hello, Mr. O'Brien." Harriet gave O'Brien a casual look. "It's nice to see you again."

"I thought we'd agreed on first names, Harriet. You're looking very pretty tonight." He grinned. "Sort of the natural, earthy look."

Harriet's laughter rang out. "That's right, Martin. That's exactly what I was aiming for."

"Well, I must say you've hit the mark. Some lucky fellow is going to have a beautiful companion this evening."

"Why, thank you, Martin. I hope he thinks so. Ashley still likes to talk a lot about Fran."

Harriet, Fran cried silently, what do you think you're doing? She bit her lip and forced herself to think calmly. Evidently, Harriet thought a little dose of jealousy might be helpful at this point. From behind O'Brien's back she shook her head in a negative gesture, signaling to Harriet to stop.

Harriet got the message, but unfortunately O'Brien turned while Fran's head was still moving. "Pesky fly," she muttered, though she had not seen a single fly inside the building yet.

Martin's eyes met hers. "Let's go," he said, his voice amused. "Beale Street awaits us."

"You be careful now," Harriet cautioned. "That's not the best part of town."

O'Brien laughed heartily. "No need to worry, Harriet, I know my way around. I did a whole series awhile back on the Beale Street renovations. People down there know me." He grinned. "*You're* more likely to get in trouble than I am—especially in that dress.'' And with that, he took Fran firmly by the elbow and led her out.

"The interview went very well, I thought,'' Fran said some moments later as he pulled out of the parking lot. "What do you think?''

"Yes, I think it did, too. But let's forget that. I want to be just Martin and Fran again with nothing bad between us. Okay?''

"Okay,'' she replied softly and was not surprised to find that his fingers had curled around her hand. "Tell me about Beale Street.''

"It runs down to the riverfront,'' Martin said. "But the most important places used to be between South Fourth and Hernando Street. Handy Park, the little park with the statue of W.C. Handy, is between Gayoso and Beale. Handy's the man who's credited with developing the blues.''

"It must have been a marvelous place in the old days,'' Fran said. "So romantic.''

Martin chuckled. "I don't know if the old-timers would say that exactly. But they tell some marvelous tales of those days. The city's trying to rebuild part of the street and make it a tourist attraction. No one is sure yet if it'll work. The street died a natural death, you see. And then general progress helped it, along with the rise of other kinds of music.

"Fortunately, the city got around to renovating before everything was gone. The old Palace Theater had already been torn down, but they saved the Daisy and the Orpheum. Shows still play at the Orpheum now.

And you can still go to Schwab's and buy old-fashioned things. It's an experience in itself."

"You have a real feel for the street," she said softly.

He shrugged. "When I decided to make Memphis my home, I found out everything I could about it." He grinned. "I did a series on that, too. I called it 'Memphis, Past and Present.' I showed the city from its founding through the yellow fever epidemics of the late 1870s, Boss Crump's administration, the founding of Piggly Wiggly Stores, integration efforts, and so on. She's a grand old lady, Memphis, but like a lot of old ladies, some of her past is not so pretty.

"But enough social history." He grinned as he pulled into a parking lot. "Tonight is for fun. Fran and Martin work too hard. Tonight they deserve to relax."

The club was small and dark, and cigarette smoke hung heavy in the air. Couples sat at little round tables barely big enough to hold their drinks, and the small space of the dance floor was packed with people. The attraction here was clearly not comfort. "Did it used to be like this?" she asked.

Martin grinned. "Worse. No air conditioning then. And everybody was out to forget their troubles."

The blare of a trumpet rose above the noise of the room and voices hushed. "Listen," Martin said.

Shivers ran down Fran's back as the trumpet wailed, reaching something deep inside her. She found the tears rising to her eyes and waited spellbound for the next perfect note.

For some minutes she sat enthralled and Martin had to tug on her hand several times before he finally got her attention. Then, wordlessly, he led her toward the dance floor and squeezed into a little space where they swayed in unison to the music of the trumpet and trombone, and the melody of the saxophone. Her body felt at one with his and synchronization techniques never even crossed her mind. When they left the place shortly after midnight, Fran felt that the rhythm of the music and the feel of Martin's body had permeated her very soul.

Back in the dorm parking lot, Martin stopped in the shadows beside the car and took her in his arms. It seemed like the most natural thing in the world, resting there against his body. "I'd like to take you home with me," he said softly. "But I can't."

She wanted to ask him why, but she remained silent. She couldn't have gone home with him anyway. He would be hurt badly when he discovered that she had used her techniques on him. To sleep with him under false pretenses was unthinkable, the worst kind of insult.

"I guess I'd better go in," she said softly, though it was the last thing she wanted. "I have class in the morning."

"Yeah, me, too."

She felt a quick rush of joy. She would see him in the morning, then, even if it was only as O'Brien. "It's been a lovely night, Martin. Thank you."

His arms tightened around her. "Thank you," he said softly. "I'd forgotten what the old Martin was like." He bent his head and brought his mouth down on hers possessively.

She wrapped her arms around his neck, pushing her body eagerly against his. Her lips opened and his tongue began to explore her mouth. She could feel the pounding of her heart and vaguely noted that his was in rhythm with it. Two hearts that beat as one: the final synchronization technique. The thought slid away. She was beyond thinking of techniques, beyond thinking of anything except how much she wanted this man, how much she loved him.

No, she told herself as he released her lips, there was no use in denying it; she loved Martin O'Brien. And the fact that she had put him in the no-win category couldn't cancel that love. It could, however, prompt her to be a little careful, she thought reluctantly. No one in her right mind invited heartbreak.

Slowly she withdrew from his arms. "I think I'd really better go."

His laughter seemed a little strained, and she could see the desire in his eyes. "Yes, I guess you'd better." He pulled her roughly back into his arms, as though he couldn't bear to let her go. This time his kiss was more demanding, and his hands began to roam over her body. Slowly, he slipped the loose neck of her dress down until her lacy bra was exposed. He cupped her breasts gently, and her body responded eagerly as she pulled him closer. She was so involved in the sensations his body was creating against hers that when he suddenly drew back she felt a tremendous sense of loss.

"Come on," he said, his voice hoarse and his eyes hard. "I'll see you back to your room. *Now.*"

Fran wanted to cry out to him not to leave her, but the words wouldn't come. Instead, she fixed her dress with shaking hands and followed him into the building.

Chapter Ten

The next morning, despite the fact that she had lain awake for a long time, her body yearning for Martin's, Fran couldn't help feeling good. The knowledge was still there, of course, in the back of her mind, that the challenge still stood, and that very soon Martin would know the truth. He would be very angry and very hurt, but maybe they could work it out. She really had not meant to hurt him. And wasn't he doing the same thing to some unsuspecting woman? Leading her on, knowing that she would be disappointed?

She pushed these thoughts out of her mind in class. They were moving right along, presenting the opening paragraphs of chapters. True to his word. Martin had come up with a book title: *The TV Interview: Or How to Bad-Mouth Celebrities and Get Away with It.* His statement of purpose, which made clear the reasoning behind the harshness of his attacks, had changed the feeling of the class toward him. They now treated him as one of the group, and that made Fran's teaching go much more smoothly.

She did wish that they weren't still pretending to be such strangers, she thought, as she and Harriet prepared for the big Friday night reception at the Peabody Hotel. She'd longed to hear her first name on his lips this morning instead of that cheerful "Miss Warren." But even under any circumstances it would not do for her to be going out with a student. That would definitely look bad to her class. And she hadn't even been able to ask him if he would be at the reception.

"Harriet, do you really think this gown will do?" Its blue softness seemed understated and she felt that she might be too nondescript, especially beside Harriet. Her gown was emerald green and she looked stunning in it, even though it was very simple and had come from the same middle-priced store as Fran's.

"That gown is you," Harriet said firmly, whirling out from the bathroom, where she'd been expertly applying makeup.

"I feel so blah," Fran moaned. "But I know those deep colors are not for me."

"Fran, honey, you look marvelous. Really." Harriet grinned. "Old Martin will be swept off his feet. Oh, say, has he ever mentioned his little girl?"

Fran forgot her gown. "What little girl?"

"I just heard." Harried frowned. "Someone told me he has a little girl. Her mother ran off awhile back and just left them both." Harriet snapped her fingers. "That's why he didn't take you home: because of her. She's only five."

And she likes the story of Tuffy the Tugboat, Fran thought. Her name is Joanie. Poor little thing...to have lost her mother in such a scandalous way. Fran's heart ached for the child, and for her father. To be so disgraced must have been very hard for a man with Martin O'Brien's pride.

And that, Fran realized, was why he hated her book. She was probably a blonde, too, the witch. That explained why he treated blondes the way he did. And you're not going to be any different, her mind cautioned. Don't make the mistake of believing he really cares for you.

"Boy," Harriet continued, "she must have been really sick to leave a man like him. Supposedly she had a thing about New York City and wanted to go there real bad. But O'Brien turned down the job offers he got, because he said the Big Apple was no place to raise a kid. I think he came from there so he ought to know." She frowned. "He wouldn't give in, so one day the wife just took off with some character who claimed he could get her on the stage. Nobody's heard of her since. This happened a year or so ago, before I moved here." She sighed. "That must have been hard on Martin. It doesn't take any expert to see that the man has a lot of pride."

Fran nodded. "Yes," she replied. "And we mustn't let on that we know any of this. Let him keep his secrets."

"Ashley didn't..." Harriet paused and looked sheepish. "I didn't mean to tell you that. Ashley told me all this stuff so I could warn you about Martin. Anyhow, Ashley said it was all common knowledge. I guess it's hard to keep things secret if you're in the limelight.''

Fran nodded and grinned. "I imagine that Ashley's version of the events was somewhat different from yours.''

Harriet dimpled. "Well, he couldn't seem to understand why Martin let his kid stand in the way of his advancement. I thought it was sort of nice myself, and I think Martin is sort of nice.''

"So do I,'' Fran said calmly. "But Ashley told you all this stuff in the hope that I would drop Martin, didn't he?''

Harriet smiled sheepishly again. "Well, that's the impression he gave me.'' She sighed. "I'm glad you don't care for him anymore, Fran. Sometimes he can be awfully selfish. And dense, too. But anyway, I thought you'd like to know these things. They might help you to understand Martin better.''

Her eyes clouded. "But honey, I'm afraid you're really going to be in hot water when Martin finds out you've been practicing on him.'' Harriet shook her head. "That man is going to explode.''

Her eyes searched Fran's. "I sure hope you've got some plan in mind, because I've never seen two people more in love.'' She paused. "Nor known two nicer people. I think you'd be really great together.''

"I do love him,'' Fran admitted softly. There was no use trying to lie to Harriet. "But I don't have a plan. I just wish he hadn't issued that stupid challenge." She signed. "And I wish I'd never accepted it. Whatever possessed me to do such a dumb thing?"

"You were mad," Harriet said knowingly, "real mad. The man can really get your dander up, and no wonder. He practically insulted you, you know." She shook her head. "No, Fran, I don't see how you could have avoided it. It was almost inevitable."

She turned curiously to her friend. "Do you suppose he suspects anything?"

"I don't think so." Fran thought back over his recent actions. "I don't think Martin is the kind of man to hide his anger, or even his suspicions. If he had any idea what was going on, he'd have said so loud and clear. I just hope I can think of something before the time is up."

"Speaking of time," Harriet said, glancing at her watch, "we'd better get downstairs. The limo will be coming to pick us up. You'll love the Peabody. It's so...elegant." She chuckled. "Too bad the ducks'll be asleep on the roof. The Peabody's famous for its ducks, you know. They march down every morning, spend the day swimming in the fountain, and march back up in the evening."

"In the courtyard?" Fran inquired absently.

"No, no!" Harriet said. "They swim in the lobby."

"You're kidding."

"No, I'm not. They live on the roof, like I said. Every morning they come down in the elevator and march down a red carpet to the marble fountain in the big main lobby, while processional music plays. And wait until you see the restaurant where Petty scheduled the party tonight. Too bad we haven't had a chance to have Sunday brunch there. They serve champagne.'' Harriet's eyes sparkled.

"Well," Fran said, still trying to get over the fact that Martin had a child. "We'd better go downstairs. It won't do to keep Mr. Pettigrew waiting. I'm sure he'll have plenty of other problems to worry about."

The Skyway Restaurant looked like something out of a fantasy. The room was circular, with tiers leading down to the dance floor where a band was providing soft music. Tiny lights were embedded in the floor and the ceiling, making the whole room shimmer. A large banquet table stood off to one side of the room, featuring a huge floral centerpiece and plates of delicious-looking food. All in all, the Skyway was something to remember.

"I'll say this for old Petty," Harriet whispered. "He knows how to do things up proper."

Fran nodded. The tiny disco lights sparkled in the semidarkness. Beyond them loomed the circular room's tall windows, which looked down on the lights of the city.

At that moment Mr. Pettigrew spied them and came bustling up. "There you are!" he cried in his usual harried fashion. "Just come over here, Miss Warren. We're going to have a receiving line by the door. Just for fifteen minutes or so, until most of the guests have arrived. We've invited some of the city's social elite so they can meet our authors."

Fran and Harriet exchanged glances. "See you later," Fran told her friend. "Have fun."

Harriet wrinkled her nose, an old gesture that made Fran want to giggle. "Don't worry, honey. I'll do that for sure."

Fran took her place beside the others, chatting pleasantly and greeting the guests. Yes, this was definitely the sort of place Mr. Pettigrew would approve of. It was, obviously, a place all the elite people were fond of.

Time seemed to pass very slowly; each time she looked at her watch, only a minute or two had gone by. Martin still wasn't there. She fought the panicky feeling that rose inside her when she considered that he might not be coming. He *had* to come, she told herself. She wanted so much to see him, to talk to him, to touch him, even though she knew she was asking for heartache. Love certainly made people act in some pretty peculiar ways, she thought. Though she knew this man was trouble, she wanted to see him and be with him, regardless of the consequences. But what would happen when the truth got out?

I don't know, Fran thought with near desperation. But I want to see him tonight. I can't help it.

"Fran." Her heart leaped and then fell again as she recognized Ashley's voice. "How are you, Fran?"

"I'm very well, thank you, Ashley." She forced herself to be civil, though her first impulse—to kick him in the shins—had been more truthful. "I'm glad you and Harriet are hitting it off so well," she said, knowing that a lie was far better than the truth in this instance. Ashley was the sort who took disapproval as a challenge. If she told him he wasn't suitable for Harriet, he would try even harder to win her friend's affection. "Harriet's a wonderful person," she added. That, at least, was true.

"Harriet's all right," Ashley said, as she tried to pry her fingers loose from his grasp. "But she's not you."

Thank goodness for that, Fran thought silently. "Of course not," she replied quietly, still trying to retrieve her hand.

Ashley hung on stubbornly. "It's you I want," he said. "Come on, Fran. Remember how good it was? We could have that again, I know we could."

She finally succeeded in freeing her fingers. "Yes, Ashley, I remember how good it was."

"Well, well." In her exasperation with Ashley she hadn't seen O'Brien approaching. "Good evening, Ashley, old man. I think I see Mrs. Singleton over there in the corner."

"I'm talking to Fran," Ashley replied pointedly, "if you don't mind."

"Oh, I don't mind," O'Brien said airily. "But I'm sure Mr. Pettigrew won't approve of your tying up the receiving line like this. Better move along."

Ashley glared, but he turned to Fran. "I'll talk to you later, baby," he said, and walked angrily away.

O'Brien smiled at her, but the smile didn't reach his eyes. "Up to your old tricks, I see."

The words took her so by surprise that she was temporarily speechless. Could he seriously believe that Ashley meant anything to her?

"Ordinarily I disapprove of working your wiles on a man," he continued, "as you well know. But that fellow deserves anything he gets. I don't think he's a fair choice, though. I don't think he dislikes you much."

"I thought we weren't supposed to discuss our conquests," she said softly. "The names are to remain secret." She wouldn't actually lie to him. But if he thought...

He shrugged. "Sure. Sure. Listen, I'll see you when this line breaks up. You can spare poor Martin a few dances, can't you?"

"Is Martin here?" she asked softly. "I thought I'd been talking to the terrible O'Brien."

His grin seemed more normal this time. "If you promise to dance with him, Martin will be here. I give you my word."

"Well, Mr. O'Brien," she said gaily, her eyes sparkling at him, "in spite of your big bad mouth and your numerous other faults, I do believe you're a man of honor. So when Pet...Mr. Pettigrew releases us from duty, I hope Martin will find me. I want very much to dance with him."

His eyes lit up and his smile grew warm. "He'll be here."

Watching him cross the room, so handsome in his light suit, she couldn't help smiling. Everything was working out—at least for this evening. Ashley's behavior might be annoying, especially when she wanted to spend all her time with Martin, but at least it gave Martin the idea that she was working on someone.

The minutes dragged by even more slowly now that Martin was here and she yearned to be with him. She saw him dancing with Harriet once and she suppressed a rush of jealousy. Harriet knew how she felt about Martin and how he felt about her.

Just when she had decided to leave the line whether Petty liked it or not, he reappeared, his necktie askew, and his expression strained. "Thank you, thank you," he murmured to them absently. "Go now and enjoy yourselves."

With a feeling of high anticipation, Fran searched the room for O'Brien's familiar figure. "Here I am," said a deep voice from behind her.

She turned. "What are you doing back there?"

"Waiting for you, what else?" He pointed to a shadowy corner near a window. "I just sat back there and waited."

"I see."

He was very close now, so close she could smell his aftershave and could hardly keep herself from walking into his arms.

"I'm glad that Martin came tonight," she said quietly.

"Me, too. Shall we dance?"

"Yes." She found her hand slipping naturally into his. "I'd like that."

The sunken dance floor was not really crowded, but it held enough people to give a comforting feel of anonymity. She slid easily into his arms, as though she had always belonged there, she thought dreamily, already succumbing to the romantic haze that had overtaken her the first time she'd danced with Martin O'Brien.

"Kind of different from last night, isn't it?" He whispered softly in her ear. She could feel the lean length of him against her, and her heart raced.

"Yes," she whispered back. "The music is different. The place is different."

He smiled down at her. "It's the company that counts, though. Right?"

"Right." There it was again. That insane feeling that everything in the world was wonderful just because she was in his arms. You're losing it, cautioned her mind. You've gone and flipped.

But Fran really didn't care. Nothing seemed to exist beyond the magic moment.

"Fran?" His whisper was almost inaudible.

"Yes, Martin?" She remember to match her tone to his.

"Remember when we were talking about the tugboats on the river?"

"Yes, Martin."

"Well, I should have told you then, but I got sidetracked."

This is it, she thought. He's going to tell me about Joanie.

"Well, the boats we saw aren't tugboats, they're towboats. There's a big difference. They don't tow anymore, of course, they push. But they're still called towboats. Do you understand?"

"Yes, Martin." Her disappointment echoed in her voice.

"Something wrong?" he asked.

"No, nothing." She hastened to reassure him, but she kept her face turned away—against his shoulder.

For a moment she'd thought he was going to open up and tell her about the child that kept him in Memphis.

It's just as well he didn't, she decided sadly. The fewer secrets he told her, the less angry he would be.

She tried to be glad about that, but it was difficult. She wanted to be close to him, physically and emotionally. And what chance did she have of that as long as his unmentioned child stood between them?

"There's something else I want to tell you," he said. "Let's go over there by one of the windows."

The view of the city's sparkling lights was beautiful, but Fran couldn't keep her mind on it. He sounded very serious.

They stood, as they had on the deck of the *Memphis Queen*, his arms wrapped around her. "The other afternoon on the river I mentioned a little girl," he said quietly.

"Yes?" She didn't turn to look at him; she didn't think he wanted her to. Her heart pounded crazily, and she hoped he couldn't feel it against his arms. Perhaps she'd been right; perhaps he was going to tell her. "Your sister's child."

"She's the reason I didn't ask you to go home with me," he said softly.

"Oh?" She tried to keep her voice noncommittal. "Is she staying with you?"

"Yes, but..." He paused and she could feel the tension gathering in his body. "But she's not my niece," he hurried on. "She's my daughter. I...have a housekeeper for her."

"I see. You've been married." She tried to keep the excitement out of her voice. He was telling her his secret, he was confiding in her. That must mean he cared a lot.

"Joanie's mother left over a year ago. We didn't get along. She wanted to go to New York." His voice became bitter. "The Big Apple is no place for a little kid. I know, I grew up there. When I turned down the network offer, she found someone else to take her. She wanted a career in New York more than anything else."

They stood silent for several minutes, gazing down at the lights of the city. Finally, Martin spoke again. "Say something, will you?"

Fran put her hands over the ones that were clasped around her waist. "I don't think that saying I'm sorry would be appropriate. Such a woman couldn't have been easy to live with."

"No," O'Brien said, his voice harsh. "She wasn't. From the very first she was a scheming, lying, cheating little tramp."

His arms tightened involuntarily around Fran and she gasped in dismay as they threatened to cut off her air. "Sorry," he apologized, his lips near her ear. "I'm still angry."

"Maybe you should..." she began.

"I am seeing a counselor," he interrupted. "I don't want to screw up Joanie's life." He sighed. "But enough heavy stuff for tonight. Martin's been asleep for so long, he wants to live it up."

She turned in his loosening arms until she faced him. "Oh? And how does he want to do that?"

His eyes darkened with desire and she felt her heart pounding in her throat.

"Well," he said huskily, "I'd like to back you up over there behind that palm tree and kiss you soundly."

She leaned toward him invitingly and he chuckled. "However, that wouldn't do."

"It wouldn't?" she asked innocently, widening her eyes. "Why not?"

"For several reasons." He ticked them off. "First, there's your professional character to consider. You have a lot of students here, and it wouldn't do to be seen kissing one of them. The rest might demand equal time."

She giggled. "Like Mr. Wilson?"

"More like Tony," Martin said. "I've seen the way that kid follows you with his eyes."

Thankfully, the darkness concealed her reddening cheeks. "Tony's just a boy," she replied lightly.

Martin laughed softly. "Maybe so. But I remember distinctly what it was like being such a boy."

"I haven't seen either Don or Tony tonight." She smiled. "I don't think that easy listening is quite their kind of music."

Martin grinned. "Thank goodness."

"You said you had several reasons," she reminded him, wishing he would throw caution to the wind and kiss her passionately right there where they stood.

"The second is our esteemed Mr. Pettigrew," Martin continued. "I think he's had enough problems for one evening."

"Such consideration is admirable," Fran teased.

"But the third and most important reason is this."
His eyes darkened and his voice fell. "If I start, I
won't be able to stop."

Me either, she wanted to say. That's the way I feel.
But no words would come out. For one long silent
moment they stared into each other's eyes, and then
he pulled her toward the dance floor. "We'd better
dance. And right now."

Chapter Eleven

Fran woke the next morning with a lost feeling. After a fairy-tale evening of dancing under the Skyway's twinkling lights, Martin had reluctantly returned her to the dorm. He had been unable to refrain from kissing her again, of course. And one kiss had led to another, leaving her so bedazzled that she had not recalled until much later that the next day was a Saturday, and therefore there would be no classes or school functions of any kind. Saturday and Sunday stretched endlessly before her since Martin had made no mention of seeing her or calling her when he had finally torn himself away.

She had slept, finally, preoccupied by the memories of that wonderful evening. No man could outdo Martin as a date; she was certain of that. But even more than his charming, courteous manner, she had loved the fact that he had talked about Joanie and their life together. She felt privileged to be allowed into the personal life of this very private man.

Well, she told herself, stretching out the kinks in her muscles, Monday and class would come, and with them would be O'Brien's cheerful if somewhat irritating smile. She grinned as she considered how he had won over the feisty Mrs. Parker, and indeed, the whole class. When he wanted to be that way, there was no one more charming than the terrible Mr. O'Brien.

A clatter sounded from the bathroom, followed by a muffled, "Darn it!"

Fran grinned. "It's okay, Harriet, I'm awake."

Harriet poked her head out of the bathroom door. "Good, I'm dying to talk."

Fran slid herself up in the bed. "Harriet Singleton, did you drop that stuff on purpose?"

Harriet's grin was guilty. "Well, maybe unconsciously on purpose. Gee, whiz, Frannie! It's already nine o'clock."

"So?" Fran grinned at her friend's use of her old school nickname.

"We're supposed to be ready by noon."

Fran eyed her friend suspiciously. "Ready for what, may I ask?"

"For the picnic, silly."

Fran stared. "Listen, Harriet, I know I've been acting kind of flaky the last few days, but I *know* we never talked about a picnic."

Harriet sighed. "Oh, that Martin. He forgot to tell you."

"Martin?" Fran suddenly felt so light-headed she thought she might float right off the bed.

"Yes. He said he'd drive us to a swimming place over the Mississippi line. I think it's called Dodd's."

"We're going on a picnic?"

"Yes," Harriet said with a grin. "You and I, and Martin and Ashley."

"Ashley?"

"Yes." Harriet looked slightly concerned. "I wanted to spend some time with you," she explained. "So I was planning it just for you and me. We would have a restful day to work on our tans. You did promise me Saturday," she said accusingly.

"Yes, I did. I remember that."

"Well, when Martin heard about it, he asked if he could come, too." Harriet lowered her voice as though someone might be listening outside the door. "I thought it would give you more opportunity to work on him." She shook her head. "Though after last night... Anyway, he looked so anxious that I told him he could come. And since I didn't want to sit there alone while you two stared into each other's eyes, I said Ashley was coming, too."

"And that didn't bother Martin?"

"Bother?" Harriet laughed. "He looked like he could cheerfully strangle Ashley. But he just smiled, kind of grim, and said he'd bring the lunch." She giggled. "He looked as though he'd like to put poison in Ashley's food."

Fran sighed and Harriet smiled anxiously. "It's all right, isn't it? I mean, I tried to tell you last night, but you were out of it. Besides, I thought Martin would mention it.''

Fran shook her head absently. "He didn't. We...we had a lot on our minds.''

Harriet chuckled. "Yeah, I could see that.''

"Harriet!" Fran warned, grabbing her pillow.

"Now, Frannie, this isn't our dorm room, remember. We have to be responsible guests,'' Harriet said, imitating one of Mr. Pettigrew's most harassed tones.

"So we do,'' Fran said, laughing and regretfully putting down the pillow. "But tell me, how's it going with Ashley?''

Harriet shrugged. "I don't really know. Sometimes I like him a lot. He's got a real sweet little-boy quality at times.'' She frowned. "But I don't like the way he uses it to get what he wants. He can be a real stinker.''

The frown disappeared to be replaced by Harriet's fun-loving grin. "But he makes good practice material, anyhow. Now listen, get out of that bed. We've got to get some breakfast, get our bathing suits ready, do our hair...''

"Do our hair to go swimming?''

"Of course,'' Harriet said impatiently. "And we have to decide what to wear over our suits.''

With a grin, Fran threw back the covers. "Breakfast first,'' she said happily. "I'm starving.''

Martin's rap on the door came exactly at twelve noon. Fran turned from the mirror, where she'd been surveying herself for the hundredth time, and hurried toward the door. Her white shorts and blouse were all right, but it had been a mistake to accept the loan of one of Harriet's bikinis. It was modest as bikinis went, but it revealed far more than Fran had expected and it seemed to be shrinking by the second.

"Good morning," she said as she opened the door. She was glad that she spoke when she did for once she got the full sight of him she felt such a rush of desire that she could hardly breathe. He was wearing a polo shirt and khaki walking shorts, and his bare legs were a deep golden brown under their dark hair. She experienced a sudden urge to reach out and touch one.

"It's actually afternoon," Martin said with a dazzling grin. "But I'll call it anything you want."

Fran returned his smile and said, "Good afternoon." When his eyes traveled down to her own bare legs, she had to resist an urge to cover herself. "I think we're ready. Harriet?"

"Right here," Harriet said from behind her. "Ready and raring to go."

"And your friend, Ashley?" Martin said, directing the question at Harriet in a way that made it clear that he was designating Ashley as her responsibility.

Harriet grinned cheerfully, her good spirits unruffled. "He said he'd go early and save us a table. It gets crowded on the weekend."

"Then let's go," Martin said, his eyes moving back to Fran. She read the message there that said he wished they were going alone. She hoped her eyes were telling him the same thing.

But Harriet cheerfully climbed in the front seat after Fran. "Let's be honest about this thing, Martin," she said, while Fran tried desperately to keep from telling her friend to shut up. "I know you'd rather be alone with Frannie." Her smile made Harriet look about sixteen. "Frankly, so would I." Absently, Fran noted that since Harriet no longer had designs on Martin, her approach to him was much better.

Martin chuckled and Fran relaxed. He seemed to have gotten over his earlier animosity toward her friend. And Harriet was growing more like her old self every day. Her brittle sophistication was fading away, revealing the fun-loving friend whom Fran loved and cherished.

"Are you always so forthright?" Martin asked.

Harriet shook her head. "No, Martin. Only with people I trust." She grinned. "I'm willing to share Frannie's company with you today. But that's as far as I'm willing to go." She leaned forward to stare accusingly at O'Brien. "After all, she and I were supposed to spend these two weeks together. You've been taking up an awful lot of her time."

"I plead guilty," Martin said solemnly. "But you've got to admit that being with Frannie is something special."

His use of her nickname made her feel young and vulnerable. His arm brushed hers as he backed the car out of the parking lot and she couldn't control her body's trembling.

"Of course," Harriet agreed. "But anyway, since I've been so good-hearted about the whole thing, I don't want you to go running off somewhere with her. Promise?"

"You should have extracted your promise before you told me I could come along," Martin said, grinning wickedly. "But seeing I'm such a fair man"—he glanced up from the road and winked at the two of them—"I have no choice but to agree."

"I knew you would," Harriet said with satisfaction. "You're a good man, Martin O'Brien. Now, shall I tell you some real interesting stuff about Frannie's schooldays?"

"Harriet!" Fran began to protest, but Martin silenced her.

"Tell me anything you want to about Frannie's past. I'm all ears."

By the time they reached the swimming place, Harriet had them both hysterical. It was going to be a fun afternoon, Fran thought, and she silently blessed Harriet. It was good to see Martin relaxed and happy. The worry lines had faded from his face and he looked young and handsome. He always looked handsome, of course, she told herself dryly.

"Down there, around the bend," Harriet directed after they had paid their admission. "See? There's Ashley's red Mustang."

Looking up, Fran saw the slight curl of Martin's lips. He disapproved of Ashley's playboy image, it seemed.

"And there's Ashley!" Harriet cried. "Sitting on that table."

As Martin maneuvered the car as close to the table as he could, Fran considered the wisdom of spending the afternoon with two men who so obviously despised each other. But it had not been her choice, really; she had promised Harriet that this Saturday would be hers.

Following her friend out of the front seat, she went around to help Martin carry the picnic paraphernalia. "You can take the blanket and the lemonade jug," he said. "I'll handle the rest."

She wanted to say something, to stop right there and step into his arms. She needed more than the casual brushing of his arm against hers. She needed the feel of his whole body against her. His eyes darkened suddenly as they gazed into hers and she turned away quickly, unable to bear the intensity of their gaze.

Fortunately, the men greeted each other politely, although stiffly, and she wondered if Harriet had given them both strict orders to behave. Her friend was capable of doing that, and of getting the desired results.

The laying out of lunch helped, giving each of them something to do. The contents of Martin's basket and ice chest surprised her. She had expected something from a fast-food store, but he opened containers of obviously homemade fried chicken, potato salad, baked beans, crispy rolls, and a huge bowl of fresh fruit salad, as well as bags of pretzels and potato chips.

"I didn't know you could cook," she said softly as she filled her plate.

"I'm afraid I can't take the credit for this," Martin replied, "though I can rustle up a pretty good meal if the need arises. This was made by Mrs. Andrews, my housekeeper. She's a real gem."

Glancing toward Harriet, Fran was surprised by a sharp look of envy on Ashley's face. It vanished almost instantly as he replied, "Yes, of course. I prefer to eat out. But then my situation is rather different."

The glance he threw at Fran was triumphant.

"Yes, I suppose it is," O'Brien said affably. Only Fran noticed the sudden tightening of his jaw. "I consider myself very lucky to have Mrs. Andrews. She's wonderful with Joanie, too."

Ashley, who had just taken a mouthful of food, swallowed the wrong way and went into a fit of coughing. Clearly, he hadn't expected that O'Brien would tell her about Joanie. Just another bad mark against him, she thought. Martin might be dangerous, but he was a man who could be trusted. Ashley was not.

They finished the meal without any further interchange between the men, and Fran forced herself to relax. Martin O'Brien was a big boy; he could take care of himself.

"Well," said Harriet cheerfully after they finished eating, "let's go lie in the sun."

"I hope you brought plenty of lotion," Martin remarked. "It doesn't look like Fran's been getting much sun."

"I haven't," she said, "but I came well equipped."

As she turned to help Harriet put the food away, she could feel the blood rushing to her cheeks. If only she hadn't listened to Harriet, if only she'd worn her own one-piece bathing suit, instead of letting her friend talk her into the bikini.

There was no chance she could stay in her shorts and blouse, either. The sun was beating down mercilessly, and even in the shade of the trees the temperature must have been near ninety. Well, she told herself ruefully, she would just have to handle it.

The food was quickly returned to the basket and everything was returned to Martin's car. Then Harriet began removing her shorts. "Might as well leave these in the car," she said cheerfully. Since both Martin and Ashley nodded in agreement and began to take off their shirts, Fran had no choice but to follow their example.

She removed her blouse first, noting that Ashley, who was in her direct line of vision, must have spent a lot of time in the sun. His dark tan looked nice on him and he had certainly kept himself in shape. His stomach had remained flat and his body firm. But she could not recapture any of the feeling she had once had for him. He was just another nice-looking man.

She stepped out of her shorts, feeling practically naked. Ashley's eyes lit up and she cursed silently. Harriet was going to hear about this.

From the other side of the car came Martin's cheerful voice. "Let's get down to the water and cool off."

"Right," said Harriet, whose bikini revealed just enough to turn all eyes in her direction.

Hastily, Fran grabbed the blanket, grateful for whatever cover she could get from it.

But her relief was short-lived. Coming around the car, she met Martin's eyes, and he seemed to see every inch of her bare skin. He grinned delightedly. "I'll say you'd better have plenty of lotion!"

"I don't burn easily," Fran said, "in spite of my fairness." She managed to get the words out over the choked feeling that came over her at the sight of him. His navy trunks revealed a flat, lean stomach, darkly tanned. But it was his chest that caught her attention.

If Martin O'Brien were allowed to conduct his interviews shirtless, she thought dryly, the whole female population would be at his mercy. It was not a weightlifter's chest, but it was well muscled. As he shifted the blanket on his arm, the muscles rippled under the cover of dark hair that curled there. Fran's fingers tightened on her own blanket as she fought the urge to reach out and touch that chest.

"Let me carry that for you," Ashley said, breaking the spell of the moment. And before she could collect her wits, he had taken the blanket from her, removing the scant protection it provided. She clutched her beach bag tighter and motioned toward Harriet, who was already moving off. "Let's go."

Down on the sand the men spread out the blankets, and a grateful Fran dropped her bag and the lemonade jug and ran for the water.

"Frannie, wait."

Against her will, Fran stopped in waist-high water and turned to wait for her friend. "I need to cool off," she said, glancing toward the sand, where Martin and Ashley were eyeing each other cautiously. "Harriet, this picnic was a lousy idea. And so was wearing this thing."

Harriet frowned. "Relax, Frannie. You look deliciously innocent."

"Innocent! Harriet..." Several heads turned in their direction and Fran lowered her voice. "I feel like Cleopatra or... I feel naked."

Harriet shrugged. "You'll get used to it, Frannie. Everyone wears them." She smiled smugly. "Even women who don't look as good as we do."

"Water feels good, doesn't it?" said O'Brien, coming up to them. "Do you swim, Harriet?"

"Not really," Harriet replied, one hand automatically going to her hair.

"And you, Fran? Do you swim?"

She saw the mischief in his eyes. "Yes," she said, giving Harriet a hard glance. "I love to swim."

"Good. Then let's go out to the raft."

"But…" Harriet began.

"You really should learn to swim," Martin said, turning his smile on her. "It's wonderful exercise."

Harriet found her tongue. "Martin O'Brien, you promised me."

"But Harriet"—Martin's tone conveyed polite astonishment—"we're only going out to the raft."

"Just for a little while," Fran added. "Here comes Ashley to keep you company." And before Harriet could reply, Fran dove into the water and headed out toward the raft.

Martin was there ahead of her, but to her surprise, he did not immediately climb up. "Come around to this side," he said as she flung back her wet hair. The water was wonderfully cool; her whole body tingled with the feel of it. Or perhaps it was Martin's nearness that made her feel so alive.

She rounded the corner of the raft. "What…" she began, but there was no need to finish the question. Martin was there, treading water, waiting for her. She moved closer.

"Come here and let me touch you," he said. "This was a crazy idea. The worst kind of torture. To see you and not be able to hold you."

"I know." The words slipped out before she could stop them, and then she was in his arms, feeling his wet body against hers. "We'll go under," she murmured as his arms closed around her.

"Just put your feet down," he said softly. "Or better yet, hang on to me." He stopped moving his own arms and she saw that the water reached only to his chin.

"Harriet could almost walk out here," she said.

"Almost." His grin remained cheerful. "Fortunately, she's not as tall as I am, and she can't see us. Now, quit talking."

Her arms slid up around his neck and she raised her lips to his. They were wet, but they were also soft and warm. She felt the wetness of his mustache against her upper lip, the surprising softness of his chest hair against her bare midriff. The feel of his wet skin was intensely erotic, and his mouth moving on hers raised feelings that the water did nothing to cool down.

When he finally released her mouth, she had to gasp for breath. But with the rush of air came her sanity. "Harriet," she reminded him. "She'll worry if she doesn't see us on the raft." He seemed about to kiss her again, and regretfully she added, "She's apt to come looking for us."

With a sigh, he conceded. "All right, all right. I wish I'd thought of this picnic. But I don't mind sharing you with Harriet." His grin returned. "Though she makes this sort of thing pretty difficult. But I don't like that Ashley." His smile faded to be replaced by a frown. "He..." Martin shrugged. "I just don't like him, that's all."

"He's an old friend," Fran said softly, reminding herself that a little jealousy was sometimes a good thing.

Martin snorted. "Some friend. A man who walks out on a woman like you? He's either stupid or crazy."

I hope you'll always feel that way, she thought silently, especially after you find out that it's your name in the envelope that Mr. Wilson is holding.

"The raft," she reminded him. "We're supposed to be getting up on the raft."

"Nag, nag, nag" he said, smiling. "Here, let me boost you up."

"There's a ladder on the other side."

"I thought you were in a hurry. We don't want Harriet to join us, now, do we?"

"No," she agreed. "We don't want that." She managed a grin, although she wasn't all that eager to leave the cover of the water.

"Grab the edge," he directed.

The next thing she knew, he had put one hand on her bikini-clad bottom and another under her foot, and had heaved her up onto the raft. She turned accusing eyes on him as he hoisted himself up beside her. "That was hardly necessary."

His grin was mischievous. "Better wave to Harriet. She's looking anxious."

Fran glared at him, but she raised herself to her knees and turned toward the shore, where Harriet was indeed looking their way anxiously. She waved and Harriet waved back, turning back immediately to Ashley. Fran smiled as she realized that Harriet had a firm grip on Ashley's bare arm.

She looked at Martin. "I can't stay out here long," she pointed out. "I haven't put on any suntan oil."

Martin frowned. "I should have brought some out with me."

"I promised this day to Harriet," Fran reminded Martin.

He shrugged. "Harriet has other things on her mind—like using your techniques on old Ashley. Although I think she might have bitten off more than she can chew."

Fran sighed. "I hope not. Ashley's not good for her."

Martin gave Fran such a sharp look that she wondered if she had touched a jealous spot. "Lie down here beside me," he ordered, stretching out on the planks. "If I'm only to have ten minutes alone with you, I want to make the most of it. I'll even keep track of the time," he added, glancing at his waterproof watch. "Five minutes to a side."

"You're such a thoughtful man," Fran said with exaggerated sweetness. "When you want to be."

"Don't tempt me," he warned, grabbing her hand and pulling her down next to him. "I feel like running off with you in spite of what I promised Harriet."

She stretched out beside him, and for the first time she really felt the hot rays of the sun.

"Come closer," he whispered, raising himself on his elbow.

"I can't get much closer," she pointed out, her heart beginning to pound.

"But I can."

She felt the cool wetness of his body against hers as he bent over her, hiding her from those on the beach. His lips were still wet and she could feel his mustache tickling her face. But his lips only brushed hers in a fleeting kiss that made her want more, much more. "Lie still," he commanded softly. "Let me look at you." He kissed her forehead, her closed eyelids, the tip of her nose, and the point of her chin.

She opened her eyes and saw his own brown ones close to hers. The water had slicked his dark hair into unruly curls, and one hung down on his forehead. He lifted a hand to touch her bare midriff. "Your skin is so soft, like satin. And your body is beautiful. But you know that"—he grinned—"showing it off in a suit like this."

"It's Harriet's suit." The words came out automatically. She didn't want to hide anything from this man. She pushed the thought of the challenge from her mind.

"It's very becoming." His finger traced the line of her chin, moved down the curve of her shoulder to the soft, exposed skin of her upper breasts. She shivered as desire rushed through her body. "And tempting," he added softly.

"You're blocking my sun." Fran had trouble getting the playful words out. His touch was doing strange and wonderful things to her.

"Good." He chuckled softly. "Then I can keep you out here longer, can't I?"

She found that her fingers had moved up to touch his chest, to toy with the damp hair curling there. Intimacy technique number two: touch him often, her mind told her. Then she pushed the thought away.

"Yes." The word was just a whisper on her lips. He bent still closer, his body covering hers, his lips moving with hers in a way that made her wrap her arms around his neck and cling tightly to him.

Chapter Twelve

Monday morning as Fran waited for class to begin she didn't know whether to sing or sigh. In spite of Ashley's effect on Martin, their picnic had been a success. But they'd come home at dinner time because Martin said he had an important date. Fran was dismayed by the jealousy she felt when he told her. Of course, he had to have some time to work on his conquest. Even a man like Martin couldn't sweep a woman off her feet immediately. Not if she had any sense, Fran thought wryly.

Fran had spent Saturday night with Harriet, who had finally succeeded in convincing Ashley that he could not come to dinner with them. By mutual consent the women had avoided discussing Martin or Ashley, and talked instead about their old schooldays.

Sunday, too, she had spent with Harriet, until Martin had called to ask her out to dinner. Fortunately, Harriet had agreed to accept Ashley's standing offer. So Fran and Martin had spent a wonderful evening alone. Every moment of it had been heavenly, including his intense kisses at the door. She had even managed to keep the challenge out of her mind most of the night.

But now, back in the classroom, she couldn't forget that in a few more days Martin would know that she had used him as a guinea pig. She knew that he would be very hurt and very angry.

As she absently watched the students entering the room, she tried to pull her thoughts back to the class. It was not fair to them for her to spend so much time thinking about Martin.

Tony came bouncing in and she smiled at him. "Morning, Miss Warren," he said, glancing around the room as he approached her. "Listen," he said, lowering his voice to a whisper as he drew closer. "I've been watching that O'Brien guy. You better look out for him."

Caught off guard, Fran mumbled, "Look out?"

"Yeah. There's something fishy about him. I think maybe he's working on..."

"Good morning, everyone." Martin's deep voice came through the doorway.

But it didn't hide Tony's last whispered word: "...you."

As the word sank in, Fran grabbed the back of her chair. "Good morning." She managed to get the words out, but she avoided meeting Martin's eyes.

Could Tony be right? Could Martin have chosen her? It made sense and it explained all the time he'd been spending with her.

Her mind raced. It would have been an excellent choice. How foolish she would look when he showed the class that he had succeeded.

But if you did the same thing to him, she reminded herself. This has got to stop, Fran thought. It's just not right. I can't go on like this, suspecting every move that Martin makes and knowing that the day of reckoning is coming.

She took a deep breath and looked around the classroom. Everyone was assembled, eager to get back to their work. And here she was, practically a basket case.

"I have an announcement to make," she said, grateful that her voice remained firm. "I have come to a decision. I deeply regret having accepted Mr. O'Brien's challenge." She was conscious that Charlie, with a newsman's instincts, had begun taping as soon as he heard the word "announcement." "On further reflection I have decided that his challenge is not only unscientific since its conclusions would prove nothing, but that it is also unethical."

She found herself looking directly at O'Brien, hoping he would understand. "To make a person fall in love with you, on a dare, so to speak, is cruel. We can't make some unsuspecting person into a guinea pig to practice techniques on, and then dash all their hopes and wound their pride by declaring publicly that it was all an experiment. It's not the sort of thing that a person whose job is healing should condone, let alone participate in.''

As she spoke, she saw Martin's face growing angrier. ''Therefore,'' she continued ''I wish to withdraw from the challenge and ask Mr. Wilson to destroy the envelopes unopened.''

From the corner of her eyes she saw Tony nod in satisfaction and she remembered Martin's observation that the boy had a crush on her. But even if Tony was wrong, even if it was someone else Martin was after, she could no longer go on deceiving the man she loved.

The realization that she loved him was not something new. But it was sharpened by her knowledge that in all probability she was about to lose him forever. ''Mr. O'Brien, will you agree to my request?''

''No.'' The word fell into the quiet of the classroom like a bomb, and Fran watched the changing expressions of her students.

''I am willing to terminate the experiment,'' Martin continued. ''But I want to know the names in Mr. Wilson's envelopes. I believe that I have won the challenge. I have made my chosen person fall in love with me.''

A murmur ran around the class and all eyes turned to Fran. At that moment she knew with certainty that one of the envelopes in Mr. Wilson's pocket carried her name. But he still didn't suspect that his name was in the other, she knew, and he was so intent on proclaiming his victory that she could not spare him.

She did try, though. "Since I've already withdrawn, Mr. O'Brien, I see no reason to subject these unknown people to embarrassment."

"I don't think we need to worry about that," O'Brien said grimly. She wondered if he still thought she had chosen Ashley.

She shrugged. "I have made all my arguments, Mr. O'Brien. The rest is in your hands."

O'Brien's eyes shifted to Mr. Wilson, who was sitting, Fran noted with pleasure, very close to Mrs. Parker. "Mr. Wilson, the envelopes, please."

Part of Fran's mind also noted that Mr. Wilson looked to Mrs. Parker for a nod of confirmation. Then, with an apologetic glance at Fran, he offered Martin the sealed envelopes.

"Would you care to do the honors?" Martin asked her dryly.

Fran shook her head. "No. This was your idea. You open them."

Martin's smile made her want to scream. "There's no need to open mine. I chose Miss Warren."

His eyes watched her closely, and she was glad she didn't flinch as the class drew a collective breath. So Tony was right. Martin had made her a guinea pig. She was aware that she was not very angry about it. It was his reaction that concerned her now.

"I think Miss Warren will agree that my old-fashioned, natural way was effective."

All eyes turned to Fran, who calmly nodded.

"In spite of Miss Warren's remarks about the unkind nature of our experiment," he continued, throwing her a glance, "I don't think there was anything wrong with my choice. She was hardly some un-suspecting innocent.'' He grinned at the class. ''And she really disliked me in the beginning. Isn't that right, Miss Warren?''

His tone was gleeful, but she replied quite cheer-fully, ''That's very true, Mr. O'Brien.''

''But now,'' he continued, ''that's all changed. Miss Warren likes me very much.'' His eyes met hers. ''Don't you, Miss Warren?''

She continued to smile. Maybe if she took this well, he would behave well, too. ''Yes, Mr. O'Brien, I have to admit that your old-fashioned charm is very effective.''

''However,'' he went on, ''I don't think Miss War-ren's choice was so fair. She chose...''

''Mr. O'Brien...'' She had to interrupt before he made himself look completely ridiculous. ''I think you'd better open the other envelope.'' She smiled at him sweetly. ''Assumptions can be a risky business, you know.''

''Of course, Miss Warren. Of course.''

She watched, her heart in her throat, as he tore open the envelope. ''Miss Warren's choice was...'' He stared down at the card, his face slowly turning livid.

The room was completely silent for what seemed an eternity. Then Harriet spoke. ''Tell us whose name it is, Mr. O'Brien. We want to know.''

With a muttered curse, O'Brien dropped the card and fled from the room. Harriet scooped it up and read aloud triumphantly, ''Martin O'Brien.''

The room exploded into a chorus of excited voices while Fran stood frozen, unable to move. Oh, Mar-

tin! her heart cried. I didn't want to hurt you. Really
I didn't.

"Well," Harriet said, taking over the class, "I think
we ought to discuss this." She turned a smile on
Charlie, who was still taping. "I mean, after all, we
were all involved in it, since the challenge was issued
here."

Mrs. Parker nodded vigorously. "I don't think the
young man should have been so upset. After all,
what's right for one, should be right for the other.
Isn't that so, Henry?"

Mr. Wilson nodded in agreement. "But Mr.
O'Brien has his pride."

"So has Miss Warren," Mrs. Parker pointed out,
starting to frown.

Fran finally regained her wits. "I guessed before he
opened the envelopes," she explained. "So I wasn't
surprised. But I'm afraid...he's so angry."

"If you love him," said Mrs. Crawford, for once
not at all timid, "you should go after him."

"But I don't know if he loves me," Fran confessed. "It could have all been because of the
challenge."

"Nah," said Tony. "I know about these things.
That guy really digs you. Mrs. Crawford's right. You
better go after him."

A chorus of assent rose from the class.

"But...but..." Fran was close to tears. "I don't
know where to find him."

"I do." Every eye in the room turned toward Charlie. "We came in my truck," he said, grinning, "and

the keys are in my pocket. So the boss has got to be out there somewhere, waiting for me."

"Where is the truck?" Fran asked, amazed at the calmness of her voice. "I've got to talk to him."

"Out that door," Charlie said, pointing. "I'll get some more comments from the class and be along later."

Fran nodded. It no longer seemed important that the whole thing had been recorded on tape, or that thousands of people might see it. The important thing was Martin and his feelings. She hurried out the door and down the hall, trying to think of what to say, how to make him understand.

She rushed through the outside door and almost collided with him as he rounded the corner of the building. He glared at her and strode on.

"Martin! Wait!"

He ignored her plea and she hurried after him, clinging to his arm. "Martin, Martin. Please listen to me!"

He stopped at last, and she stood panting beside him. "What for?" he growled. "So you can play some more tricks on me? No, thanks, Miss Warren." He spoke her name so sarcastically that she winced.

"I've been suckered once too often." He glared at her, his chest rising and falling with the force of his anger. "So breathe in time with me," he taunted cruelly. "Or stand like I am. See just how far it'll get you."

"But, Martin..." She clung to his arm with both hands.

"Martin is dead," he said flatly. "Your deception killed him. I should have known better than to let some broad get under my skin. You're all alike."

Her own anger began to rise at the unfairness of his reaction. After all, he was just as guilty as she was. And when he used that despicable word "broad," she let herself go.

"Well, well, Mr. O'Brien, aren't we being just a little high and mighty? You seem to forget that you did the same thing to me. And it was your stupid idea." She still clung to his arm, but she gave him the extent of her anger. "You tricked and deceived me. You lied to me about your important date. You tried to humiliate me in front of my class, in front of hundreds of viewers. And you have the gall to yell at *me*."

"You weren't straight with me," he muttered. "I hate that in a woman."

"And I suppose you were straight with me?" she inquired crisply, hope fluttering in her heart. If she could just keep him talking.

"I told you about Joanie."

At least his tone was lighter and he was no longer trying to jerk his arm away. "Not right away, you didn't."

"I let you see my private self," he insisted.

"So did I," she returned.

"I was beginning to feel…"

"I did feel," she said firmly, forgetting all about the rules in her book. "I felt that I loved you, that you loved me. But I was obviously mistaken. You don't want to behave like a mature person. Of course it hurt when your wife ran off but you shouldn't let that poison your relationships with all women. Ashley dumped me." She used the nasty word on purpose. "But I haven't gone around since hating all men."

She let go of his arm and drew herself up to her full height. "I was waiting for the right man and I thought I'd found him. But if you're going to behave like a spoiled child and blame all this on me, then maybe you're not the man I thought you were."

She took a deep breath and hurried on. "I even tried to save you from embarrassment by withdrawing from the challenge. But you had to play the big hero and pound your chest in victory. You brought the whole mess on yourself."

She was breathing heavily now, as heavily as he, and the two of them stood glaring at each other.

"I made you love me!" he shouted. "My methods worked!"

She was past caring what she said now. "And I made you love me!" she screamed back. "My techniques worked!"

He shook his head stubbornly. "No, I don't."

"You don't love me?" Her heart was pounding in her chest.

"No, I don't," he repeated. Even though the words were yelled at her, they seemed to carry little conviction. It was now or never, she thought.

"Fine. Great." She spat the words at him. "That just completes the picture of the terrible Mr. O'Brien. I might have used my techniques on you, but I wasn't playing games. I really loved you. But you...you set the whole thing up to make me look like a fool. Well, you've succeeded. Congratulations, Mr. O'Brien. And good-bye.''

She swung on her heel, half blinded by sudden tears. If he really didn't love her, there was nothing more to do. And if he did, the next move was up to him. She tried to think which way to move, where she could go hide herself and let the tears come.

But she had only gone a few uncertain steps when he grabbed her arm and swung her around to face him again. "I do love you," he moaned. "God help me, I do." And he pulled her into his arms and kissed her frantically.

When he released her mouth, he kept his arms around her. "You fight a good battle," he said cheerfully, his anger gone. "I'm afraid that's a quality you may need."

"Why?" Her anger, too, had faded and she felt wonderfully alive and happy. Whatever had been wrong between them, they could work it out.

"Well, being married to me could be a trial."

"I'll say." Charlie's voice issued from behind a clump of nearby bushes. "You've got him now, Fran," the cameraman said gleefully. "I've got the whole thing on tape."

"Charlie." Martin's frown threatened to return.

"I thought it'd make a nice wedding present," Charlie said innocently.

Fran laughed. "As far as I'm concerned, it would make a great show. But maybe you'd better just announce that we've both withdrawn from the contest."

Martin smiled. "Maybe I'll just announce that my old-fashioned methods worked. They're still the best."

"You can't prove that," Fran returned. "My techniques are tried and tested. They worked on you."

Martin shook his head. "No, it wasn't your techniques, my love, it was my methods."

"It was my..."

"Kiss!" Charlie yelled, becoming temporary director. "Kiss now!"

And they did, laughing, while Charlie recorded it all, happy to be taping the world's most unique wedding present. But, he told himself with a smile, as their kiss went on and on, this was probably the point where he should slip quietly away, leaving the lovers alone. And he did just that.

author **JOCELYN HALEY,**
also known by her fans as **SANDRA FIELD**
and **JAN MACLEAN,** now presents her
eighteenth compelling novel.

With the help of the enigmatic Bryce Sanderson,
Kate MacIntyre begins her search for the meaning behind
a nightmare that has haunted her since childhood.
Together they will unlock the past and forge a future.

Available at your favorite
retail outlet in **NOVEMBER.**

DREAM—02

COMING NEXT MONTH

PLEASE STAND BY—Marie Nicole
Cartoonist Dirk Kilpatrick had created "Abby," the perfect woman.
No one could compete with her...until he met Vinnie. She had all
Abby's charms, with one advantage...she was real.

FORGOTTEN LOVE—Phyllis Halldorson
Could love conquer all? Mercy's husband, Morgan, had lost his
memory, and she was a stranger to him. Perhaps wrapped in her
arms he would remember the love they'd shared.

THE MATTHEWS AFFAIR—Victoria Glenn
Denise's past had left her as skittish as a colt when it came to love,
but Logan wouldn't give up. Slowly he aimed to win her heart.

WITH MARRIAGE IN MIND—Dorothy Cork
Noeline Hastings had resigned herself to marrying her reliable but
boring boyfriend, Andrew. Then she met Justin Fitzroy and realized
that she could never settle for another man.

THE SEA AT DAWN—Laurie Paige
Roth wasn't the kind of man to fall for a woman like Melba. He
was rich and powerful. He wouldn't be attracted to a sensible,
down-to-earth girl...or would he?

CAMERA SHY—Lynnette Morland
Calm, cool and unerringly professional, Carla Copeland had met
her match. Fletcher Arendt sensed the passion lurking beneath her
facade, and he planned to find a way to unleash it.

AVAILABLE NOW: